Born in Meknès, Morocco, in 1958, **Abdelilah Hamdouchi** is one of the first writers of police fiction in Arabic and a prolific, award-winning screenwriter of police thrillers. He is the author of *Whitefly* and lives in Rabat, Morocco.

Translator **Jonathan Smolin** is the author of the critically acclaimed *Moroccan Noir: Police, Crime, and Politics in Popular Culture* (2013) and the translator of *Whitefly*. He lives in Hanover, NH.

D0533146

The Final Bet

Abdelilah Hamdouchi

Translated by
Jonathan Smolin

hoopoe
AN IMPRINT OF AUC PRESS

This paperback edition published in 2016 by
Hoopoe
113 Sharia Kasr el Aini, Cairo, Egypt
420 Fifth Avenue, New York, 10018
www.hoopoefiction.com

Hoopoe is an imprint of the American University in Cairo Press
www.aucpress.com

Exclusive distribution outside Egypt and North America by I.B.Tauris & Co Ltd.,
6 Salem Road, London, W4 2BU

Dar el Kutub No. 25802/15
ISBN 978 977 416 779 9

Dar el Kutub Cataloging-in-Publication Data

Hamdouchi, Abdelilah
       The Final Bet / Abdelilah Hamdouchi; translated by Jonathan
    Smolin.—Cairo: The American University in Cairo Press, 2016.
          p.   cm.
          ISBN 978 977 416 779 9
          1. Arabic Fiction –Translation into English
          2. Arabic Fiction
          I. Title
          892.73

1 2 3 4 5   20 19 18 17 16

Designed by Adam el-Sehemy
Printed in the United States of America

1

AMONG THE DOZENS OF RESTAURANTS spread out on the Ain Diab coast, Sofia's was the only one with an air of simple elegance, as if it reflected the personality of its namesake. Most of the restaurant's customers were summer tourists or French people who lived in Morocco year-round. It was rare for locals to come and enjoy its coq au vin, soufflés, and escargots.

The last customers of the night left the restaurant around ten o'clock. Business was slow in the fall, except on weekends. Sofia switched off the neon sign outside and locked the door early so she could spend a little more time with her son Jacques, who was on his last night of a weeklong visit.

Besides Jacques, at the dinner table was Michel, a dear family friend who was an advisor at the French Cultural Center. Next to him was his slender wife Catharine, who had a freckled face and short hair. There was Claude, who worked at the embassy, and his Moroccan wife, who had brown skin and blue eyes. Her name was Fatima, but friends called her Fati. As for Othman, Sofia's husband, he was adding up the receipts at his desk in the corner, as he did at the end of every night. He was very uncomfortable sitting there, not because he was tired, but because he had been trying to make a phone call for more than an hour. Whenever he reached out to pick up the receiver, he felt his wife's gaze cut across the room at him. He was terrified of her catching him.

"Chéri, who are you talking to?" she'd inevitably ask.

Othman was tall and thin; he had a body exuding masculinity. His dark eyebrows increased the firmness of his eyes. He had a thick mustache, which he brushed often, and an artificially contemplative air. The impression he left on others—and especially women—was that he was a man who symbolized virility and could overwhelm any rival.

Five years ago, poverty was the biggest problem in Othman's life. But now, he wore expensive Italian clothes and drove the latest model BMW. He ran a fine restaurant in the chic Ain Diab district and lived in a magnificent villa in Anfa, the most exclusive neighborhood in Casablanca. All this comfort was thanks to his French wife Sofia, who was also the source of his misery. The main reason was their age difference: Othman was thirty-two years old and bursting with strength and vigor, while Sofia was seventy-three. The obvious disparity shocked everyone, especially when they found out this old lady was the wife of such a vibrant young man.

Othman's frustration at not being able to make the call caused his hand to shake on the adding machine. He was taking a long time with the receipts, hoping Sofia wouldn't ask him to join them yet again. He looked at his watch and saw it was midnight. Sofia and her friends danced, sang, and exchanged jokes, as they did all night long. As far as Othman was concerned, they were just making noise. Their loud, horrible laughter pounded his ears as he sat at the desk. His only solace was pretending their outbursts were nails being hammered into his wife's coffin. For an hour now he used his work as an excuse to stay behind the counter, hoping to make the time pass faster. But here was Sofia, opening another bottle of Beaujolais, filling their glasses, and singing old songs from the days of her distant youth.

She was happy. No one could see any trace of suffering on her face, despite her advanced age. Also, her figure was deceptive: from a distance, it gave her the appearance of a young woman, especially when she was wearing tight pants, as she was tonight. Her blond hair hung down on her bare shoulders.

Sofia was only afraid of two things in life: the first was death, which made her do everything she could to stay healthy and fit, and the second was Othman cheating on her. Because of this, she'd keep a close eye on him everywhere he went, scrutinize the features of his face, and listen closely to the inflection of his voice. Maybe she'd catch the trace of another woman on him. She knew Othman was a terrible liar. Whenever she caught him in some white lie, he turned into a shy boy who confessed in no time.

Through his half-closed eyes, he saw her coming toward him, dancing and holding two glasses of wine. She normally didn't drink more than a glass a day, but tonight she was having more fun than usual. Sofia was acting like a young girl, letting herself get carried away. Her face was full of joy.

Othman took a deep breath trying to get a hold of himself. He smiled at her, pretending to be annoyed at all the work he had to do. She pushed one of the glasses toward him and caressed his fingers.

"Chéri, have you finished yet?" she asked gently.

"And you?" replied Othman tensely.

Looking him in the eyes, she took a sip from her glass and put it on the counter. She then ran her fingers through her shiny hair, provoking him with a look full of desire.

"Chéri, we're celebrating. This is Jacques's last night. Come join us. We didn't have enough customers tonight for all this bookkeeping."

Othman didn't have the strength to look at her. A loud crashing sound coming from the kitchen saved him. As soon as Sofia stepped away to see what happened, he seized his opportunity. He quickly picked up the phone and dialed. After the first ring, he heard Naeema's voice on the other end, full of anxiety.

"Othman? How could you leave me outside all alone like this?"

"I haven't had a second to call," he said quickly, whispering as softly as he could. "I've tried for an hour to tell you not to wait for me. They're taking much longer than I thought."

He hung up without hearing Naeema's response. Sofia suddenly came back from the kitchen.

"Something wrong?" asked Othman quickly, trying to preempt any questions.

"This Abdelkader, chéri, we've got to do something about him. Or get rid of Rahma."

She stopped herself, not wanting to ruin her mood.

"Come, my love, let's dance," she continued softly.

She swallowed what was left in her glass and put on her favorite song, "To All the Men I've Loved Before." Othman felt much better now that he told Naeema not to wait for him. With the skill of a professional actor, he passionately wrapped his arm around Sofia's waist, showing her the vigor of a real man. He drew her close to him, spun her around, squeezed her tightly, and then pushed her away before yanking her back to him again.

"Let me go, please let me go!" she yelled out, giggling like a child on a seesaw.

Her son Jacques got up, staggering a bit. He was fat; he had a strong face and a short frame. Jacques was twenty-three years older than his mother's husband.

"For God's sake, get away from my mother!" he said jokingly.

The others broke out laughing until Fati began coughing after she got a piece of olive caught in her throat. Jacques approached Othman, imitating a knight with a sword in his hand. He dismissed Othman with a light shove on the chest.

"Madame wants to dance with me," he said grandiosely. "Calm yourself and retreat."

Othman lifted his hands as if afraid of a duel. He stepped back, while Fati continued coughing.

"What a night!" she said a few times as she tried to clear her throat.

At Mohammed V Airport in Casablanca, most of the arriving passengers were coming from Europe. As soon as they got off their plane, they realized they didn't need their jackets. The hot weather no doubt surprised them; even though it was the end of November, the daytime temperature was in the upper seventies, though at night, the dazzling sun disappeared and a chill set in. During the week he spent in Casablanca, Jacques got a light tan, which would no doubt be a source of pride once he got back to the miserable Parisian weather.

They were standing near the border police and for several minutes Jacques embraced his mother like a child not wanting to let go.

"Poor Jacques," said Michel, the close family friend who insisted on going with them to the airport. "He's so delicate and sensitive."

Othman looked impatiently at his watch without bothering to respond. The way Jacques held onto his mother seemed shameless. Even after she stepped away from him, Jacques kept holding her by the shoulders, treating her like a lover.

"I don't want to leave you, Mama."

Sofia laughed and turned to the others as if trying to lighten Jacques's farewell.

"We'll see you next summer, right?"

"Of course, Mama."

"Oh, chéri," she replied.

Finally letting go of Sofia, Jacques gave Othman a firm handshake.

"Watch after my mother," he said, smiling.

"Of course, my son," said Othman.

Michel laughed so hard he caught the attention of some travelers. Othman's response was ridiculous. Jacques was old enough to be his father.

There were about five people waiting in front of the border post. Sofia didn't want to leave until she saw her son cross through passport control. After ten minutes, which Othman and Michel endured resentfully, Jacques's turn came. But, in a gallant gesture, he gave his place to a pregnant woman and waved to his mother and the others, telling them not to wait for him any more. His mother blew him a kiss, took her husband's arm, and turned around to leave.

As he did every night after he got home from the restaurant, Othman took their dog Yuki out for a long walk. He smoked a cigarette as he strolled in the middle of the road among the grand villas. The neighborhood was calm. There was a line of tall palm trees on either side of the street, the base of each tree ringed by a patch of trimmed grass. The air was so crisp and cool that Othman zipped up his jacket.

When he reached the square, he was overwhelmed by anxiety. He looked at his watch. It was eleven o'clock. She broke her promise, he thought; she's not here like she said. She waited for him here inside her car almost every night. While Yuki ran and played, they'd sit together, talking and embracing each other. He remembered her sweet lips on his and felt crushed that he wouldn't see her tonight. The thought of returning to the villa without the rejuvenation Naeema gave him was unbearable. He could already feel the torture he'd face once he got home. Where would he get the strength to deal with Sofia without seeing Naeema?

He took out his cell phone and looked around to see if anyone was watching. As he dialed the number, Yuki was running around happily.

"Hello, Naeema?" he said anxiously, almost holding his breath. "I managed to get out here early. . . . I'm at our usual place. . . . No, Naeema, this isn't the time to fight. I'm sorry about yesterday. . . . I can't tomorrow afternoon. I need you now. . . . Please . . . . In the morning I have to run errands and work at the restaurant. . . . Fine, tomorrow at the same time. Good night."

He then turned toward Yuki.

"Come here, you dog!" he yelled out bitterly.

When he got back to the villa, Othman let Yuki loose into the garden and then went in the house. He walked straight to a small bar in the corner of the living room, took out a bottle of whiskey, and filled a glass. He emptied it in two gulps, making his eyes tear up. He then filled his glass up again.

From the bedroom above, Sofia's voice came down to him softly, full of desire.

"Chéri. . . ."

Without these glasses of whiskey, he'd never be able to bear having sex with her. He thought she was intent on torturing him. He had to hide his resentment and disgust and approach her with excitement and burning desire. He'd embrace her with tenderness, pampering her and whispering sweet words of love in her ear. He had to force himself to get used to her favorite positions, pretending to love them while praising her body, which was full of splotches like leopard skin and made him sick. After she'd finally climax, his disgust would last for hours as she lay there in bliss. He'd have to keep holding her and repeating words of love and gratitude.

"Chéri, come lie next to me," she cooed as he walked up to her.

When he entered the room, she slowly pulled the blanket off her. He could see her dried-up breasts emerge from the opening of her silk kimono. The features of her face seemed fixed, almost artificial. He turned his back to her as he took off his clothes, not wanting her to watch him. He had to get himself ready, feverishly thinking of Naeema's naked body. If Sofia saw he couldn't get it up, it would turn into a double torture session. She'd keep asking him what was wrong and wouldn't let him go to sleep until he revealed his deepest feelings. He had no choice but to endure it all, doing whatever he could to dispel any suspicion of the utter loathing she inspired in him.

There were only eight people in the restaurant tonight. Most of them drank a lot of wine but ordered just a few appetizers. This annoyed Sofia and she complained that they thought she ran a bar and not an upscale restaurant. As for Othman, this lull in business made him happy. At ten thirty, he told everyone they were getting ready to close and tried to hurry them out. His wife didn't seem to notice that her husband was in such a rush.

Sofia opened the kitchen door and inadvertently caught her cook with his hands on Rahma's full hips. She was in the middle of washing dishes. Instead of yelling at Abdelkader, Sofia went straight to the dirty plates, picking them up and inspecting them angrily. She stared at the two disdainfully and slammed the dishes down in the sink.

"Everything's dirty!" she screamed at Rahma. "Why do I have to yell to get you to do things right!"

Her eyes lit up with anger as she looked over at Abdelkader. He happened to be gripping a butcher knife and seemed hesitant to put it back with the other knives.

"Don't get so angry, Madame," he said faintly. "Everything's fine."

She hated him and knew he was jealous of Othman. At the same time, she couldn't fire him since he was such a good cook. Before Rahma, she had to get rid of two female workers because of Abdelkader. He was a ladies' man. He had been married twice and was responsible for five children, not all of them born in wedlock.

After the restaurant closed, Sofia sat in the car near the front entrance waiting for Othman. She was smoking a cigarette and listening to Mozart as she usually did when she was angry. She saw all the workers leave from the side door and pile into an old Renault 4 parked nearby. After a bit, Othman left too. He locked the front door and hurried over, getting into the driver's seat next to Sofia. He turned on the ignition, but as soon as the car started, he got out without saying a word, as if he just realized he had forgotten something. He went back in the restaurant as the Renault 4 drove off.

He walked straight over to a box under the desk and took some money from it. All of a sudden, he heard several metal pans crash to the ground in the kitchen. Othman then heard another noise he couldn't quite make out. Surprised and a little scared, he carefully approached the kitchen door and noticed it was ajar. He heard a cat meow, a sound that seemed odd to him, almost eerie. He stood frozen for a moment, deciding whether to go in the kitchen or not, and all of a sudden, he heard the car horn outside. Othman let out a sigh, chuckled, and quickly left the restaurant.

In the bedroom, Sofia sat in front of the vanity, taking off her make-up with pieces of cotton. She then put a special cream on her face, looking closely at the wrinkles no cosmetic surgery could fix. She was paying special attention to her appearance tonight; she had on a silk nightgown and a beautiful cloth wrapped around her head. The mirror didn't reflect her youthful spirit, but a body in need of some help. Sofia wasn't the kind of person to torture herself, however. For her, the body was independent of the spirit and her spirit was youthful, even if the mirror said something entirely different.

She slipped under the covers like a small child. It annoyed her that she was always the first to bed and that she had to call out to Othman several times to get him to join her.

Finally, Othman stood at the bedroom door and smiled at her cheerfully. It didn't take her long to realize he wasn't coming to bed. Her mood took a turn for the worse.

"Coming to sleep, chéri?" she asked, already knowing the answer.

"I have to take the dog out," he muttered without looking at her.

"But I already walked him today."

Did she know why he left the house every night?

"I like taking him for a walk after work."

After a moment of silence, she smiled indulgently.

"Don't be late, chéri."

He knew under this calm demeanor, she hid her displeasure. Once he got out on to the empty street, he let Yuki off the leash. He lit a cigarette and walked quickly, almost working up a sweat. If she breaks her promise tonight, he thought, he'd go crazy. He had never felt as lonely as he did right now.

As he approached the square, he saw her simple Renault 5 parked in the usual place, under the tallest palm tree. He was overwhelmed with happiness and relief. He looked around to make sure no one was watching and slipped into the front seat next to Naeema. Besides the huge age difference between her and his wife, Naeema looked more European than Sofia. She was fair-skinned and had honey-colored eyes. Her hair was fine and long; she pulled it back in a ponytail like a twenty-year-old Moroccan college girl, even though she was twenty-seven. Naeema had a magnificent body, especially her legs. Othman met her at the sports club where his wife worked out. Sofia was actually the one who introduced them. Naeema was Sofia's aerobics instructor.

Othman leaned close to give her a passionate kiss, but Naeema didn't respond. She pushed him away, and all he could do was give her a quick peck on the cheek.

Was she crying while waiting for him? He understood how difficult her situation was. A single girl in an empty street at such a late hour. Not only was it dangerous, it was a matter of respect and honor. She looked like a prostitute sitting in her car like that.

They sat there without looking at each other, silent for some time, melancholic. He knew she didn't want to be the one to start talking.

"Was I . . . late?" he stammered.

"No, but I almost died waiting here for you all alone," she replied in a soft voice, trying to hide her emotions.

He reached out and put his arm around the edge of her seat.

"No one would touch you in this neighborhood."

"Is the old lady asleep?" she asked, raising her voice a bit.

"Can she fall asleep without me next to her?" Othman said with a slight smile.

She suddenly smacked her hand on the steering wheel in rage.

"Sorry," she said insincerely.

Othman knew how tense she was. He laughed cheerfully, hoping to melt her icy demeanor.

"I didn't come to joke with you," she said. "I'm here to resolve this situation. My patience has run out."

Othman pulled his arm away.

"How long have you been waiting?" he said, trying hard to speak calmly. "Two years? I'm the one who's had to endure it for more than five."

"I wasn't in your life five years ago," she said, looking at him resolutely. "I'd bet everything I have that old lady won't die until she's a hundred. You've got to see her at the club. She's got the health of a mule. The young girls can barely finish my class but when she's done, she goes straight on to the next one. If you're counting on her dying soon, God help us!"

Othman smiled coldly and turned away from her. He watched Yuki for a few seconds as he chased a torn ball around. He knew what was on Naeema's mind. He was usually lucky enough to make her forget the details. He hadn't ever felt the possibility of a breakup like he did right now. He was blind with love for Naeema. She was incredibly beautiful. And she loved him too.

"We have to embellish reality," he said. "If you want, I'll divorce her tomorrow, but then everything would be lost. You want an unemployed lawyer as a husband?"

"If this whore stays alive for another twenty years," she said, "I'll wind up waiting for you until I become an old hag like her!"

Even though Naeema always told him not to smoke in her car, he suddenly realized he had a cigarette in his hand.

"We've talked about this a thousand times. I thought we agreed to put it off."

"My patience has run out!" she screamed in his face, tears welling up in her eyes. "I can't bear it anymore."

She began sobbing. Othman felt like he might lose her altogether. Looking at her crying like this, he thought she was about to end it. He wondered how he could sacrifice the love of his life for a shriveled up seventy-three-year-old woman who acted like a child. He felt sick to his stomach and suddenly lost his desire to hold and kiss Naeema.

"I've got to go," he mumbled without looking to her.

"You want granny? Then go."

She turned on the ignition before he got out of the car and took off with a screech as soon as he shut the door.

Othman lit a cigarette. He crushed the empty pack in his hand and tossed it away. His heart began beating sharply and his throat became dry. His lips quivered like he was about to break out in tears. He thought he'd go crazy as he asked himself over and over again why he had married Sofia. He remembered how she had saved him from miserable poverty. But wasn't it his right to live with the woman he loved? Didn't he deserve happiness? He felt his world being ripped apart. Sofia was old and worn-out; she'd been sucking his blood for over five years. She controlled everything about him and made him live in isolation. Because of the way he felt about being seen with her, he avoided his friends, family, and everyone else. Othman was terrified of the ridicule in their eyes and their looks of pity. He hated Sofia. Every night, as he held her lying in bed, he imagined himself putting an end to it and killing her.

2

WHEN THE PHONE RANG, DETECTIVE Alwaar was on the verge of nodding off. He stayed in the other room studying horse betting numbers and chain-smoking until he slipped into bed next to his wife after midnight. He hadn't yet picked the numbers he'd bet on. He happened to be dreaming of his favorite horse losing the race when the phone rang.

Who's Alwaar? If he got the chance to introduce himself, he'd probably just say he's been a criminal detective for thirty years, but was never lucky enough to get promoted to commissioner. His real name was Allal ben Alawaam. The inspectors under his command called him Alwaar, "rough guy," but this nickname soon went beyond work and took on another meaning, one with a political connotation. That's because Alwaar and a group of cops like him rejected the recent reforms curbing police violence. Times were changing quickly in Morocco and the government was now calling for the end of torture-related deaths in police custody, opening up investigations into police misconduct, and arresting cops implicated in human rights violations.

The response of some on the force, at first, was to stop taking crime-fighting initiatives, show indifference, and watch things from a distance. This led to increased crime on the street and soon left its trace on public opinion. People were beginning to lose faith in the police reforms, linking the sharp rise in violence and continuing human rights abuses to what they saw as the inability of Moroccans to respect the rule of law.

This difficult transitional period made Alwaar feel out of place. His work became confusing; it was hard for him to get confessions without slapping or kicking a suspect or sending them down to the torture room in the basement of the police station before interrogation. Alwaar didn't know how to do his job without brutality. He just couldn't get used to sitting in front of a suspect without being aggressive or insulting, talking to them like they were in some smoke-filled café. He had to crack the whip.

For a whole year he didn't do much of anything. He simply put in his time, dreaming of days past. It was in this difficult period that he discovered racehorse betting and got addicted to it. Yet little by little he started getting used to the new situation in Morocco, especially when he cracked a few cases. He had to obey the winds of change, even if with little faith or slack enthusiasm.

On this night, as he was finally about to fall asleep, the phone saved him from seeing his favorite horse lose the race. Alwaar waited to pick up, hoping it would stop ringing on its own. But when the phone kept at it, he knew the call was work-related. He leaned on his pillow and turned on the bedside lamp. He watched his wife as she turned to the other side of the bed, pulling the covers over her head so the light wouldn't bother her. Alwaar picked up the receiver but didn't say anything. The voice on the other end shook him awake as if he was facing some sudden danger.

"Sir," the voice said without the usual greetings, "this is Inspector Assou from the nightshift. We just got news a foreign woman was murdered in her home."

Alwaar grimaced as he got out of the warm bed.

"Who reported the crime?" he snapped, almost chastising the inspector for what happened.

"Her husband."

"The address?" said Alwaar coldly.

"Villa Sofia, number twenty-three, Zuhour Street, Anfa."

"Tell the DA," he said in total resignation. "And tell Inspector Boukrisha to make sure no one touches the body until I get there."

Alwaar put the receiver down, breathing heavily. He used to smoke more than two packs a day of cheap Moroccan cigarettes and now had problems breathing. He had a chest exam recently, and the doctor told him to quit smoking immediately. The only thing Alwaar could do was get by on a pack and a half a day instead of two or even more.

He walked, exhausted, across the bedroom and opened the closet. When he was undressed, Alwaar looked like a retired boxer. He had a puffy face and bags under his eyes. His features made him look feeble and his lifeless eyes never seemed to focus on much of anything.

As he put on his suit, his wife stirred in bed.

"What's so important they had to wake you up?"

"A woman . . . foreign . . . was murdered," he replied, out of breath, as he knotted his faded necktie.

With a mechanical movement, Fatima sat straight up as if she hadn't just been deeply asleep. She was maternal, the mistress of the house in the strictest sense. She was skilled at cooking, washing clothes, and cleaning. Her favorite pastime, however, was gossiping with the other women in the building. For years she'd been the official spokesperson on everything concerning Casablanca's security. Tomorrow morning, before even preparing breakfast, she'd spread the news of this shocking crime among the women of the building, promising them details on the next installment.

Alwaar finished putting on his suit and adjusting his pale red tie. He then took his gun from its hiding spot in the middle of the folded clothes in the closet and tucked it into his belt. Fatima looked at him closely with a hint of compassion.

"What happened to the commissioner's promise of giving you a desk job until you retire?" she said, getting up.

Alwaar waved his hand in a motion of resignation.

"They always do this when something big happens. They make the rounds and call everyone. In the end, I'm the only guy they find. The young detectives don't have enough experience for them."

"All this trouble," she grumbled, helping him put on his coat, "and they haven't even promoted you to commissioner."

Did she mean to strike at his most vulnerable spot? Alwaar took a few steps back, narrowly avoiding her foot. He just couldn't hide his anger whenever the subject of his promotion came up. He seemed confused and irritable to her.

"What good would being commissioner do me?" he asked, searching for something in the pockets of his thick coat. "My days at work are numbered. At my age, people only ask for health and well-being."

That was his way of easing his grief and hiding his bitterness. But, in truth, even the mention of not getting promoted incensed him and made him feel as though all his dreams had gone up in smoke. Old age seemed like a poisoned coldness slowly creeping toward him.

He continued rummaging in the bottom of his pockets.

"If you're looking for your notebook, it's in front of you on the table," said Fatima, as if settling something obvious.

She followed him to the door and after he left, she turned the locks, reconciling herself to being alone.

She never guessed her children would grow up so fast, get married, and vanish into thin air. Their oldest son lived in France, while his brother was a cop—like his father—in Meknes. As for their daughter, Samiya, she had also gone into the same line of work as her father. Last year she passed the academy's entrance exam on the first try and was now training at the police academy in Kenitra.

Alwaar stopped his Fiat Uno directly in front of the police car opposite the villa gate. He looked at his watch before heading in. It was quarter after one in the morning. He stopped to breathe in the clean air of this high-class neighborhood and then walked toward the gate where a uniformed cop was standing. The cop greeted the detective with an official salute but Alwaar didn't even look at him.

The first thing that struck Alwaar was the vast size of the villa's garden, which was illuminated with powerful lights that made it look like the middle of the day. The grass was bright green and perfectly trimmed like the artificial turf on a sports field. The edges were lined with multicolored flowers and in the distance there was a deep blue swimming pool just like one in a luxury hotel. The non-stop barking put Alwaar on edge so he rushed toward the house. Once inside, he felt like he was in a castle. A magnificent crystal chandelier adorned with traditional designs hung from the ceiling. There was a marble fountain in the middle of the entryway, and the ground shone with polished marble that made you feel sorry for walking on it, no matter how expensive your shoes were. All the furniture was refined and revealed a foreign taste with Moroccan touches.

Inspector Boukrisha hurried over to him with his round belly sticking out. He appeared older than his age, though he was twenty years younger than Alwaar. He had a brown face and curly hair, but it was difficult to pin down the exact color of his eyes. He constantly exaggerated his gestures to reinforce his naturally hoarse voice.

"The crime took place in the bedroom," he said excitedly.

The detective started walking toward the stairs, but was stopped in his tracks by the sight of a man hunched over on a leather couch with his face between his hands and his chest trembling.

"Who's that guy?" said Alwaar, winking at Boukrisha. The inspector cracked a smile that confused the detective.

"The victim's husband."

Down the second floor was a wide hallway with a number of doors, all of which were well-lit. On each side of them were tables with antiques and vases, together with more decorative chairs than quite fit the space. The bedroom was at the end of the hallway. It was a wide room with two wardrobes and a vanity. There was another door inside leading to the ensuite bathroom. As for Sofia's body, it was lying on the bed drenched in blood. Her nightgown was open at the waist. Her right arm was extended as if she wanted to grab something. The left hung down to the ground. She was lying on the edge of the bed and looked like she was about to fall off, but death had frozen her in this position. Alwaar stared at her pale aged face and understood the meaning of the inspector's ambiguous smile. He looked for Boukrisha among the other cops in the room.

"The young guy downstairs, that's her husband?"

Boukrisha nodded his head with a stunned look on his face.

"He's the one who called in the crime?" asked Alwaar.

"Yeah, he's the one," said Boukrisha, trying to clear his voice.

The detective's eyes widened and he moved his head slowly. He asked one of the cops—an enthusiastic young man who'd joined the force only two years ago—to stop taking photos. Alwaar moved back and examined the body from the different corners of the bedroom.

His first step was to verify that the crime scene hadn't been tampered with. He especially wanted to make sure the murder weapon, a knife covered in blood next to the corpse, was in the same position they found it in. The detective had the forensics officer take a close-up of the knife. Alwaar then scanned the bedroom floor, which was covered with a beautiful Moroccan carpet. He saw a framed picture near the bedside table. He bent over and examined the photo without touching it, so as not to compromise any potential fingerprints.

When he straightened up, he felt a light dizziness. He pressed his hands on his temples and took a deep breath. The room was swarming with men: Boukrisha, the forensics agent, three inspectors, and a team of ambulance men who were crowded at the door, ready to take the body away.

Alwaar moved to the window and opened it. He looked out onto the calm, beautiful street, trying to get a hold of himself. Whenever he carried out the initial stages of a murder investigation, he felt a strange heaviness, a kind of distraction impeding his determination.

For Alwaar, this was the most difficult stage of any investigation. He'd look for what the evidence was telling him and read it from every angle before moving to the next step. This made Alwaar move slowly, testing the patience of his assistants, who were always standing around, awaiting orders.

He finally got down to business. He walked toward the bedside table and, with a cloth wrapped around his hand, opened the top drawer, taking out a box lined with silk. He opened the lid and found it full of jewelry: gold earrings, a diamond necklace, and a ring with a sparkling jewel. He immediately ruled out theft as a motive for the murder. This sped things up. He then looked into the bathroom and was transfixed. He wasn't searching for clues, as much as he was dazzled by its splendor: there was a wide bathtub big enough for a giant, gleaming white towels in an elegant arrangement, a bunch of nightgowns hanging on hooks, and dozens of creams, combs, oils, perfumes, soaps, and shampoos.

Near the entryway downstairs, Othman was still sitting in shock. His eyes were red from weeping and his lips were taut. He was sighing deeply and having trouble breathing. Soon, he managed to get a hold of his trembling.

Alwaar walked down to Othman and sat in front of him, taking out his notebook. Alwaar gave him the once-over before introducing himself.

"I'm the homicide detective in charge here and this is my assistant," he said, pointing to Inspector Boukrisha. "You're the victim's husband?"

Othman nodded without having the strength to look into Alwaar's eyes.

"Name?"

"Othman Latlabi."

"Your wife's name?"

"Sofia Beaumarché."

"Her nationality?"

"French."

The detective took his time writing down the information in his notebook. This gave him the chance to check out Othman again.

"Fine," said the detective in an irritated tone. "Tell us what happened."

Othman closed his eyes and took a deep breath. He stammered more than once before finally starting talking.

"We got home from the restaurant around eleven. Sofia went up to the bedroom ahead of me. I took the dog out for a walk. When I came back," he said, breaking out in a fit of tears, "I found her like that."

A feeling of weakness overwhelmed him and he started weeping out loud. The detective observed him in a cold, professional way. Othman got up, grabbed a box of tissues, took one out, and wiped his eyes. As he moved to sit down, he almost fell over.

"Calm down," said Inspector Boukrisha impatiently. "We know this is hard for you but we've got our job to do."

Othman stared at the inspector.

"You said you found her like that," Alwaar pressed him.

Othman was having a hard time talking. He gave the two men a miserable look.

"She was barely alive," he said, doing what he could to continue. "She was on her last breath and tried to speak. She opened her mouth but no sound came out. I was terrified. I didn't know what to do. I knew she was going to die. She motioned to a photo of her son she had in her hands, almost like she wanted to say goodbye to him. She tried to hold onto it but it fell. I was shocked and confused. I screamed out and my entire body started shaking. I've never seen a murdered person before and I hate seeing blood. When I got hold of myself, I saw she was still moving and I immediately called for an ambulance and the police."

The detective looked up and exchanged a glance with the inspector, who was standing with his elbow on the edge of the large fireplace. Alwaar took something down in his notebook.

"Listen, Othman," he said in an official tone. "I'll be straight with you. You're the only one who knows what happened. You've got to remember all the details."

Othman grimaced as his eyes widened.

"That's it. I told you everything."

The detective felt Othman's story didn't check out. There was clearly something wrong with the knife. It wasn't normal for killers to leave the murder weapon behind at the crime scene, unless something forced them to. Also, the knife wasn't still in the victim's stomach; someone pulled it out and left it next to her on the bed.

The detective swallowed with difficulty. For him, the murder weapon was always the fundamental clue in discovering the killer. And this point was shrouded in obscurity.

The technicians finished their work. Alwaar ordered them to leave and had the ambulance men take the body to the morgue.

"I want to call one of her close friends," said Othman, stammering.

After thinking for a moment, the detective nodded in agreement. Othman went to the phone on top of the small bar in the corner of the living room, picked up the receiver, and dialed the number. The other end rang for a while. He almost put the receiver down when someone finally picked up.

"Hello? Michel? I'm sorry to wake you," he said in a rattled voice. "I have terrible news. Sofia was just murdered. I was outside walking the dog and when I came home, I found her in the bedroom . . . stabbed to death. . . . Yes, the police are here with me now. Will you tell Jacques?"

Othman hung up. He then opened a nearby glass cupboard and took out a big copper lighter. He lit a cigarette and sat down again.

"Who's Michel?" snapped Boukrisha.

"A close friend of Sofia's who's an advisor at the French Cultural Center."

Alwaar took the information down in his notebook.

"And Jacques?" he asked without raising his head.

"Her son. He was here last week and went back to France."

His eyes filled up with tears again. He put his hand on the back of his head and then stroked his mustache nervously. He gave the impression he was living a nightmare. The detective looked at him closely, trying to figure out what Othman was really feeling. Was his grief genuine or was he struggling to hide the truth?

"What time did you take the dog out?" Alwaar asked, starting up a second line of questioning.

"Around eleven-thirty."

"When'd you get back?"

"About half an hour later."

"Did you meet anyone while you were out? One of the neighbors or anyone else see you?"

"No, I don't think so," said Othman, hesitating. "I stayed in the square with the dog. I played with him for a bit and then came back. The street was completely empty."

"Do you usually take the dog out?"

"Every day, except Saturday and Sunday."

"When you came back, how'd you find the door of the house?"

"Just as I left it. Locked."

"You forgot to close it when you went out?"

"No. I'm sure I locked it."

"Fine," said Alwaar, looking at his notebook. "The motive for the crime wasn't theft. The proof is that your wife's jewelry is still here."

Instead of putting out his cigarette in the ashtray, Othman crushed it with his foot on the ground, clearly irritated. Alwaar watched him closely.

"There aren't any signs of a break-in on the windows or doors. How'd the killer get in?" asked Boukrisha roughly.

Detective Alwaar didn't like this question. He gave Boukrisha an annoyed look.

"Do you have other valuables here besides jewelry?"

Othman didn't seem to get the question.

"Do you keep any money here?" he added to be clear.

"No. We leave the daily take from the restaurant there."

"Where's the restaurant?"

"Ain Diab."

The detective asked for more information about the location. He soon figured out where it was.

He needed a cigarette, but he never let himself smoke during an interrogation. He stared at Othman and then went through a number of ideas in his head. He came to and resumed his routine questions.

"Who lives with you here?"

"No one. It's just me and my wife."

"What about a maid?" asked Boukrisha, trying to keep Othman talking.

"There's Rahma but officially, she works in the restaurant. She comes here every morning to do some housework."

Boukrisha sat down on the edge of the couch, putting all his weight on his knees. He wanted to ask Othman if he had kids, but then remembered Sofia's age and felt the question would be insulting. They have a dog, Boukrisha thought disdainfully.

The detective turned over a new page in his notebook. After a moment of silence, Othman relaxed a bit. He seemed to think the questions were over. As Othman sat there, the detective looked up more than once to keep an eye on him.

"When'd you marry her?" he asked finally.

"About five years ago."

"How'd you meet her?"

Othman sat up suddenly. Did the question shake him? He hesitated for a bit before answering.

"Through her ex-husband."

The two men suddenly became interested. They waited for Othman to go on but he seemed reticent.

"Was he Moroccan too?"

"Yeah, from my neighborhood. Unemployed like me. He was an immigrant in France. He married Sofia there and convinced her to come to Morocco and open up a restaurant."

The detective looked around the huge entrance area thinking Othman wasn't going into enough detail on his own. He had to be pushed.

"Why'd they get divorced?"

"They had a misunderstanding."

"About what?"

"What happened—" Othman hesitated as he took out another cigarette, "was that she caught him here with another woman."

"The first husband was a lot younger than her?"

Othman felt embarrassed and lowered his head. He had hoped the line of questioning wouldn't go in this direction. Despite what Othman wanted, this point was too juicy for the detective to ignore.

"Fine," said Alwaar after Othman didn't reply. "You met your wife through the ex-husband who was from your neighborhood. How'd it happen?"

"He didn't introduce me to her," Othman said firmly, as if denying an accusation. "But he did tell me about their life together. And I knew she liked young men. Once they got divorced, I tried and it worked out."

Boukrisha smiled mockingly.

"Her first husband's still here in Casablanca?" he asked in his hoarse voice.

"No. He has a business in Marrakech."

The detective flipped through his notebook quickly.

"And the son, Jacques, the one you had your friend tell about the murder, how about him?"

Othman lit another cigarette with the big copper lighter, which let out a high flame. He exhaled the smoke and looked anxiously at the detective.

"When she was young, she had a French husband. He died in a car accident."

"Her son's the one in the picture we found on the ground?"

"Yes," said Othman timidly.

The detective stared at him with a look of disgust. He realized Sofia's son had to be a lot older than this husband of hers who was sitting in front of him.

"You said he visited recently. . . ."

"Yes," Othman said, cutting him off. "He went back to Paris a week ago."

The detective clearly looked tired. He yawned in an unseemly way and then ground his dentures. He closed his notebook, got up, and started circling the couch.

"Who do you think had a reason to kill your wife?" he asked Othman directly.

"I don't know," Othman replied in a wavering tone.

"You took the dog out for a half-hour walk," said the detective, going over the basics. "When you returned, you found your wife murdered. There wasn't a break-in or any sign of forced entry. There isn't anything stolen and you don't suspect anyone."

He continued moving slowly around the couch.

Othman remained frozen with the cigarette burning between his fingers.

"That's enough for now," the detective said suddenly after thinking for a moment. "I'll be waiting for you in my office tomorrow morning."

He took out his card, held it up before Othman, and put it down on the edge of the fireplace. Boukrisha got up, staring aggressively at Othman. It was hard for him to end the interrogation like this, without any resolution. If the detective left the matter to him, he would've openly accused Othman of the crime.

"You didn't see anything and you didn't hear anything?" growled Boukrisha in Othman's face. "You don't have any idea what happened?"

Othman ignored him and got up to walk the two out. Once they were in the garden, Alwaar looked over at the dog that was barking earlier.

"A German Shepherd, right?"

"Yes," replied Othman tersely, hoping to end the ordeal.

He said goodbye to the two cops in front of the villa gate. He then turned off the garden lights, went back into the house, and threw himself down on the couch in the living room. He sat up suddenly and his eyes widened. He then lowered his head and hit his fist against the wall, cursing over and over again.

The Fiat Uno didn't move from its spot in front of the villa gate. Detective Alwaar sat in the driver's seat with Inspector Boukrisha next to him. The two of them were smoking in silence. It was almost three o'clock in the morning. Boukrisha was yawning repeatedly, hoping Alwaar would let him go home to bed. But Alwaar was taking his time thinking about the case. The idea of heading home to sleep didn't even cross his mind.

"You forgot to tell him when to come see us tomorrow," Boukrisha said, just about out of patience.

"I didn't forget," replied the detective in a sharp voice. "It was on purpose. We've got to give him space to see how he'll act."

"You're going to put him under surveillance?" asked Boukrisha, trying to keep his eyes open.

"Of course. Who do you want to partner with?"

Boukrisha tossed his cigarette butt out the window. His red eyes betrayed signs of irritation and anger. The last thing he wanted to do was spend the rest of the night slouched in his car seat keeping tabs on some villa. The detective picked up the radio receiver and called central for a couple of men to take over. He found only one inspector free. Alwaar told him to meet them at the scene immediately.

"Hundreds of disasters and all we've got are a handful of cops," he said, annoyed, putting the receiver back down. "You've got to get some sleep. I'm going to need you tomorrow."

Boukrisha was relieved. Ten minutes later, a run-down Renault 4 without any sign it was a police car pulled up behind the Fiat Uno. The driver turned off his lights, got out, and hurried over to the Fiat. Alwaar told him to get in the backseat.

Inspector Asila's buddies called him 'Anxiety.' At fifty years old, he lived alone on the roof of a crummy building. Three years ago, he declared bankruptcy and divorced his wife. He left the house to her and their four children. Since he could no longer afford to support them, he began a new life. All his friends were afraid he'd wind up asking them for money.

Alwaar filled him in on the crime. He told Asila to keep an eye on the house and make sure he stayed awake.

"I slept great this afternoon," said the inspector.

"Good. You've got to keep this villa under surveillance. If the guy inside leaves, call central immediately. Follow him and let us know what he does. Understood?"

"Yes, sir."

"Good night."

Asila chuckled. He got out of the Fiat and went back to his Renault 4. After the detective and Boukrisha took off, Asila stayed awake inside his car, smoking at times and singing to himself at others. He kept thinking about his family tragedy, feeling terrible for his kids. He was full of resentment at his stubborn ex-wife. He was also furious about his job. He worked day and night for a crappy salary that never went up. After twenty years of service, being a cop didn't even give him a respectable quality of life.

Just before dawn, he started to get so tired he got out of the Renault. While he was pissing behind the car, he looked out on the high-class street with its lofty palm trees and magnifi-cent villas. They looked like the houses of Hollywood stars.

Asila felt like he was in another Morocco, one that need-ed different cops. He was thinking that the maids' rooms in these castles around him were a hundred times better than the shitty place where he lived on the building roof. He became more and more frustrated so he decided to sit back down in his car. He closed his eyes, convinced he'd start feel-ing better if he just relaxed a bit. He didn't notice that he was beginning to fall asleep.

3

THE MORNING SUN HADN'T YET come up on the rooftops when Othman left the villa. He happened to look over at an old Renault 4 parked nearby and, through the predawn light, could make out someone sleeping inside. It didn't occur to him this person was supposed to be keeping him under surveillance.

He walked slowly under the palm trees in the middle of the road breathing in the sweet air. He hadn't slept much and hadn't even bothered to change his clothes. He spent the rest of the night on the couch, going through different ideas in his head, smoking one cigarette after another. He knew this day wouldn't be like anything he'd ever experienced before.

Once he got to the main street, he waved down a taxi and slipped into the back seat. He told the driver to go to Derb al-Fouqaraa. His parents' house was located in the Derb's alleys, which were teeming with hundreds of families crammed together in old buildings. Their houses were so damp people had to take their things outside every day to dry them in the open sun.

Othman became more and more anxious as the taxi neared his parents' house. Once they arrived, he paid the driver and got out. As he walked down the narrow street, he lowered his head, looking down at the ground, hoping not to have to say hello to any of the neighbors. He knocked on his parents' door quietly and after a minute, his mother answered. She was surprised to see Othman standing there so

31

early in the morning. She stood frozen, unsure if his visit meant good or bad news.

Othman was so eager to get inside he walked past his mother, closing the door behind him. It wasn't even six o'clock in the morning. He could tell his knock on the door had woken her.

His mother was a heavy-set woman. She had on several layers of clothes and a couple of scarves on her head. She had an exhausted face that bore an expression of concealed pain. She'd been suffering from rheumatism for years.

"Where's Papa?" asked Othman with a sigh, throwing himself down on a nearby chair.

"He went for morning prayer. He's not back yet."

She looked at him with the heart of a worried mother. She sat opposite him and folded her arms across her chest.

"What happened? May it be good, God willing."

Othman tried to tell her the news calmly but he couldn't hide the shock on his face. His voice quivered and he felt like he was free-falling into a deep abyss.

"Sofia's dead, Mama. She was murdered."

His mother looked at him as if she didn't believe a word he said.

"Murdered? Who murdered her?"

"I don't know."

His mother noticed him trembling. She could see the panic in his eyes.

"And the police?" she asked, staring at him with a strange look. "You told the police?"

"They interrogated me all night. I'm in trouble, Mama."

He put her hands between his and kissed them over and over, crying like a child. His mother pushed him away suddenly.

"Why are you in trouble, my son?" she yelled, her voice shaking with terror. "What'd you do?"

"I found her on the bed, Mama," he said, hesitating and trying to get a hold of himself. "She was in a pool of blood with a knife in her stomach. She tried to speak. She opened her mouth but couldn't say anything. She pleaded with her eyes, looking down at her stomach, begging me to pull out the knife. I couldn't refuse her so I did it. I was totally confused. Sofia let out a moan and closed her eyes. I thought she was dead so I began to scream. I was in a state of complete shock. When she moved again, I realized she was still alive. I jumped up and called an ambulance and the police."

The panicked look in his mother's eyes abated. Othman could tell she didn't understand the problem.

"So why are you afraid, my son?" she said, trying to calm him down.

He hesitated before confessing what was torturing him.

"Maybe I left my fingerprints on the knife when I pulled it out of her stomach."

He knew from her confused look she didn't know what the fingerprints might mean. She barely had an elementary school education.

"If they find my prints on the knife, they'll arrest me and accuse me of killing her," he added in a firm voice.

His mother finally understood the seriousness of the situation. Grief-stricken, she suddenly slapped her face.

"But my son, you have a law degree in French! Why'd you touch the knife when you knew these fingerprints might get you arrested?"

"She begged me, Mama. I couldn't ignore her as she was lying there dying."

He stood up, at a loss, and started pacing around the room.

"But maybe the prints were damaged. I could've wiped them off," he said, as if talking to himself.

"The killer's a thief!" his mother screamed. "Break-ins have been going up these days. Yesterday, they killed a man for ten dirhams. The poor guy was coming home from the mosque after morning prayer."

"No, Mama," said Othman, walking back and forth nervously like someone possessed. "They didn't steal anything. All her jewelry's still there."

His mother became more and more aware of the trouble her son was in.

"So who killed her?"

"I don't know," he said in complete despair.

He sat back down obsessing about the prints, hoping they couldn't be recovered from the murder weapon.

When he heard a knock at the door, his hair stood up. He was terrified the police had come to take him away. He calmed down when he saw his father walk in with a carton of milk and four Moroccan doughnuts covered in sugar and tied together by a thick piece of green grass.

His father was a bit older than sixty. His skin looked dried out; his face was wrinkled and his body was bony. He spent most of his life watching people's cars on the street for spare change. Othman threw himself on his father and hugged him tightly as if he'd just come back from a long trip.

Othman launched into what happened and his father listened intently as he wrapped his jalbab around his legs absentmindedly and pressed down on the Marrakech-style skullcap that hid most of his bald head. He stayed silent as he listened to his son.

"Why'd you grab the knife?" he said finally in an accusatory tone. "If someone else did that, we could've said he didn't know what he was doing. But you spent four years at the university studying law!"

"She begged me, Papa!" said Othman, as if struck by a heavy blow. "You can't refuse someone who's dying."

"And the police?" said his father with a hint of bitterness. "What'd they do with you?"

"They asked me some questions and told me to come to the station today."

Othman's father slapped his hands together.

"I knew things wouldn't end well with that whore. May God curse greed and everything that comes with it."

Othman felt defeated. Why was his father intent on insulting him at a time like this?

"God willing, the police will arrest the killer," said his mother, trying to intervene. "Everything will be fine. I'll make breakfast for you. It will all turn out well."

The father bowed his head and fell silent. He never allowed his emotions to show on his face. But this time, his tears got the better of him.

"Tell me the truth, son," he muttered quietly in a hoarse voice, not without a certain suspicion.

"Why do you think so badly of me?" Othman yelled, choked with pain, as he jumped up out of his chair.

Before his father could speak, Othman ran out of the house, which shook as he slammed the door behind him.

Inspector Asila was dreaming of holding the pop singer Madonna in his arms when he started hearing loud noises around him. As he woke up, he saw a group of kids with backpacks on their way to school. One of the kids looked over at him through the driver's window and stuck his tongue out. Asila cursed at him as he sat up. He looked at his watch and saw it was quarter after nine. How long had he been asleep?

Asila looked over at the villa gate scowling, trying to calm his agitated nerves. He opened the window and filled his lungs with the fresh air. He kept his eyes on the police radio and checked to make sure his gun was still in its holster.

At the end of the street he saw a woman coming toward him. When she was only a few steps away, he could tell she was about thirty years old. She had a scarf covering her hair and wore a jalbab and shoes with worn heels that made a clicking sound on the pavement. She stopped at the villa gate and looked over at Asila in the car. She then hit the buzzer.

The inspector swallowed and sat up, trying not to waste much time figuring out what to do. The woman kept ringing the bell, looking quickly over at him several times. The inspector noticed that her patience began to run out. His cop instinct told him she wasn't used to waiting outside like this.

He left the car and started walking toward her. As he got close, he noticed the skin on her face was still smooth. Her withered eyes, however, had the look of misery typical of Moroccan maids.

"Anyone inside?" he asked innocently.

"Who are you?" said the woman, looking at him in confusion.

The inspector ignored her question and hit the bell. The only reply was the dog's barking.

"And who are you?" he asked, scrutinizing the woman's face with his unadulterated police stare.

"I work here," she said automatically with a hint of fear.

The inspector pressed on the bell again and began to realize the difficulty of his position.

"What's your name?" he asked gruffly.

"Rahma," she answered nervously. "And you?"

The inspector knew he'd be in big trouble if the guy inside had taken off while he was napping in the car. He needed this woman's help.

"I'm a police inspector," he said roughly in an attempt to scare her. "Police. Is there another door?"

Rahma's face went white as she shuddered.

"There's one in the back. What happened?"

Asila stared her down until she lowered her eyes.

"You don't know?"

Her heart began beating faster.

"No."

"Your boss was murdered yesterday," he said after hesitating a bit.

Rahma placed her hand over her mouth, stricken with grief. Her cheekbones protruded as her jaw dropped. She was on the verge of tears.

"He must've fled from the back," said Asila to himself.

Rahma couldn't believe what she heard.

"Fled? Who fled?"

Asila stepped past her and held the buzzer down. He pulled on the door handle violently but all that did was stir Yuki up. The dog became more agitated and started barking viciously.

4

OTHMAN WANDERED THE STREETS FOR about half an hour, feeling resentful about all the help he'd given his parents over the past five years. He thought about the gifts he'd bought them and the cash he gave them every month. He remembered how he'd held his father's hand as they went to a travel agency, surprising him with two tickets for the hajj, one for him and the other for his mother. That was followed by a ridiculous controversy that raged in their family for days about whether his parents' hajj was legitimate since the money came from a Muslim marrying a Christian woman. His father gave in only after consulting a faqih.

Othman walked around so immersed in his thoughts he didn't hear all the noise around him. He remembered the money he gave his brother, who was six years younger than him. It was enough cash for his brother to set up a TV shop. Thanks to Othman, his brother married a girl he fell in love with and is now living a life of ease, stability, and comfort. His brother falls asleep every night in the arms of his young, beautiful wife. As for Othman, he lies in bed at the end of the day like a cold hard statue holding a bag of bones covered in leopard skin.

He felt like a total failure as he wandered among the tall buildings in the morning sun. He found himself thinking about his wretched childhood, which he spent between studying at school and making money selling plastic bags on the streets or carrying people's bags at the market. The only thing he could remember about his teens was misery. He slaved for long hours as a waiter in dingy cafés or cleaning filthy cars at the bus station where his father worked.

Despite all the work and deprivation, he stuck to his studies, without the least encouragement or help from anyone. He was smart and did well in school without much effort, even though he felt like it was just a place for him to relax between his arduous jobs. When he began studying at the university, however, he was struck by terrible low self-esteem. He was so shy he barely had the courage to steal glances at girls. To escape his loneliness, he threw himself into his studies, spending almost all his time at the library, dreaming he'd become a great man some day. Getting his law degree, however, earned him nothing but unemployment. And once he was a university graduate, he no longer had the strength to work miserable street jobs like before.

What his father said this morning shocked him. Othman still couldn't believe it. It's true that despite their poverty, his parents didn't encourage him to marry Sofia. They never visited him at his villa and they never invited Sofia to their home. They were afraid of the neighbors' mockery and scorn. He remembered his mother's reaction when she saw a picture of Sofia for the first time. She sighed, slapped her cheek, and said: "Good Lord, my son, you're marrying a woman who's older than me!" Despite all that, they didn't explicitly tell him not to marry her. And their unease soon turned to delight once the money started coming in.

Was he wrong to have married her? Before meeting Sofia, he used to stage sit-ins in front of the parliament building with all the other unemployed university graduates. And after the boots of the police trampled him and his back was almost broken under their clubs, he stopped protesting, convinced that jobs were handed out only through personal connections and corruption and not by protesting or staging sit-ins. He then got the idea of emigrating to Europe illegally through the Strait of Gibraltar like all those boat people, but he didn't have enough money to pay the smugglers. When he met Sofia, he thought Europe immigrated across the Strait to him. And when they got married, he could rest easy knowing he did everything he could to save himself. He suffered horribly when he was unemployed for four years; every imaginable door was slammed in his face. Even the idea of suicide tempted him from time to time. Sofia was his last chance.

Othman decided to grab a taxi before the traffic jams began, as they usually did this time of morning. After a short ride, the car stopped in front of a modern building on al-Jabal al-Dhahabi Street in the upscale Maarif neighborhood. He paid the driver and got out without bothering to take the change. He went in the building and walked up the stairs quickly to Naeema's apartment on the third floor. He closed his eyes as he pressed the bell, feeling an exhaustion that went beyond simple weariness. When she opened the door for him, he saw the house was still dark. He must have just woken her up.

Naeema was fidgeting with her nightgown. She didn't even straighten her hair before opening the door. He looked at Naeema and thought she was even more beautiful without make-up. Othman threw himself into her arms and embraced her tightly. He breathed in the sweetness exuding from her body. She was barely able to push him away from her so she could close the door.

She looked at him, feeling a sudden panic.

"What's going on?" she asked with a confused smile on her lips.

Othman walked into the living room and sat down. He took out a pack of cigarettes, lit one, and exhaled the smoke.

"Sofia died yesterday," he said in a trembling voice. "I found her murdered after I got back from seeing you."

Naeema let out a laugh as if she'd just heard a joke.

"Are you serious?"

"She was stabbed to death in the bedroom," he said insistently.

She scrutinized him intently and her face went pale.

"Who killed her? Thieves?"

"Nothing was stolen. Her jewels were in the drawer. Nothing's missing."

"So who killed her?" she asked, wide-eyed.

"I have no idea," he said in a quivering voice.

Naeema left him for a moment and opened the window. Sunlight flooded the room. She went to the kitchen and came back with an ashtray that she put in front of him. She sat down staring at him, waiting for more details. She noticed he was scared and agitated.

"Was she killed when I was with you?" she asked trying to conceal her nervousness.

"That's what I said. After you left, I went back to the villa, walked up to the bedroom, and found her on the bed with a knife in her stomach, covered in blood."

Suddenly, he stopped talking. Should he confess his fear about the fingerprints? He thought that would horrify her. And she might think he's the one who did it. He decided to wait, especially since he couldn't remember if he wiped his prints off or not. Why rush telling her?

She looked at him searchingly. His paleness scared her.

"Did you call the police?" she asked in a suspicious tone.

"I called the ambulance first but she died before they got there."

"And the police?" she asked with a hint of fear.

"Yeah. A detective named Alwaar wore me out with all his questions. I haven't slept at all. I've got to go to the police station in a bit."

She looked at him and lowered her head as she rubbed her eyes.

"So who's the killer if it wasn't thieves?" she asked without looking up at him.

"Nothing was stolen," he replied, doing everything he could not to burst into tears. "And the police have ruled out theft as a motive. I'm going to be their prime suspect until they find the real killer. If only I told them the entire truth yesterday."

Her eyes widened with fear.

"I didn't kill her, Naeema," he added in a hoarse voice. "Believe me. I just wish I told them I was with you when the murder took place."

He thought again about the prints and almost confessed his fear about them to her but he stopped himself.

"Are you going to give my name to the police?" she asked with her lips trembling.

"I have to tell them the truth. You're the only proof I have that I wasn't at the villa when she was murdered. I can't lose you as an alibi."

She grimaced as she suddenly flung her long hair back.

"That could get us in trouble. Our relationship will come out and maybe. . . ."

"But isn't it the truth?" he cut her off sharply, provoking her with an angry stare.

"You're innocent," she hurried to say, trying to calm him down. "So why rush to tell them about us? That might lead to other things, know what I mean? Wait a bit. Maybe they'll arrest the killer today or tomorrow."

"And if they don't? There's a good chance they'll arrest me when I go see them today."

She paused and then put her hand over her mouth as if trying to stop herself from screaming. Othman saw tears well up in her eyes.

"Are you afraid for yourself?" he asked cautiously.

"I'm afraid for both of us!" she said, breaking out in tears. "But what do we have to fear? You're innocent. You didn't kill her."

He dropped to his knees, wiped her tears, and kissed her submissively on her forehead. He then wrapped his arms around her and his own tears began to flow.

"I didn't kill her, Naeema. I didn't do it."

He fell silent and started rocking back and forth slowly. He felt a strong urge to go straight to the police to declare his innocence. He got up suddenly feeling a powerful sense of terror. The fingerprints! Once again, he gave in to his cowardice and weakness. He felt overwhelmed.

"I'll make coffee," said Naeema, trying to avoid terrible thoughts. She wiped away her tears and smiled at him.

Before she went to the kitchen, a strange idea hit her.

"Maybe God wanted us to be together," she said. "So He sent an angel to kill her."

Othman closed his eyes not knowing what to make of what she said. He wanted to take off his shoes and lie down on the couch to sleep, just for a few minutes. But his nerves were shot and he didn't have the strength to be alone, so he joined her in the kitchen. He sat on a chair near her and spread his hand out on the small Formica table. Naeema had her back to him as she put the pot on the stove. He checked out her svelte athletic build and her blond hair that hung down to her shoulders. He thought about how he could see her magnificent neck when she pulled her hair back.

"She was supposed to have a workout with me today," Naeema said, taking a jar of fruit preserve out of the refrigerator. "She'll miss class for the first time. She was a very devoted student."

Othman wasn't amused.

"Hurry up with the coffee," he said, looking at his watch. "I've got to get to the police station."

"Are you going to tell them about me?" she asked, trying to hide her fear.

"Depends on what they ask."

"If they call me down there, what do I say?"

"The truth. No more, no less."

She looked at him quickly as the jar of preserve almost fell from the counter. Othman caught it and pushed it back. He stood up, took Naeema by the shoulders, and shook her, staring into her eyes.

"I'm warning you, Naeema. However things turn out, only tell them about us. Don't say anything more, okay?"

She nodded her head and bit her lips. She was so scared she felt like she might pass out then and there on the kitchen floor.

5

ALWAAR GOT TO THE STATION about eight thirty in the morning and was told the commissioner was waiting for him. The detective found the office door ajar and the commissioner talking on the phone. Without stopping his conversation, he motioned to Alwaar to sit down. The commissioner was a huge man with a piercing stare. He didn't make any decision before pondering it over and over again. He always doubted people and trusted only a few of his assistants. At the top of them, however, was Alwaar.

The commissioner put the phone down and leaned back in his big leather chair. He sat opposite Alwaar, looking at him without saying a word. With his typical slowness, the detective gave the commissioner a detailed report on the case. Between one sentence and another, the commissioner nodded his head in approval of the steps the detective had taken.

The commissioner didn't offer any commentary at first and simply stared at Alwaar.

"There's no doubt her country's embassy will stick their nose in our affairs," said the commissioner finally, warning the detective. "You've got to do clean work. You said the prime suspect at this point is the husband?"

"I left him under surveillance while we complete the investigation."

Someone suddenly knocked on the door and came in. It was Inspector Asila. He was in a pathetic state. His hair was mussed and his eyes bloodshot. His face was pale as if he had just been slapped. Asila didn't know if he should apologize for barging into the commissioner's office in such a disrespectful way or just start talking.

"You didn't tell me the villa has a back door, sir," he told the detective, trying hard to clear his throat.

Alwaar knew immediately the inspector was in a jam.

"What happened?" he asked sharply.

Asila's voice rattled as sweat dripped from his forehead. It was obvious he didn't have the courage to tell the truth.

"Start talking!" the commissioner yelled out in a rough voice.

"I was keeping the front gate under surveillance while the target fled from the back," said the inspector all at once after collecting his breath.

A moment passed and all Asila could hear was the detective grinding his dentures in suppressed rage. Alwaar grabbed the inspector by his arm and squeezed it forcefully.

"Admit you fell asleep and didn't notice when he snuck out!" he screamed.

The commissioner's face went pale.

"How many men do you have on surveillance?" he asked the detective.

Alwaar was startled and squinted his eyes.

"I only found Asila for the job. It was after three in the morning."

The commissioner banged his fist on the desk and shook in his chair. The detective hesitated before replying and looked at the commissioner as if apologizing.

"How do you know he fled?" he asked the inspector.

"The maid came to the villa as she usually does every morning and rang the bell several times," he explained, looking past the detective at the commissioner. "No one opened the door. I was then forced to approach and when we gave up on someone answering, I asked her if there was another door and she said yes."

"Get out of my face!" yelled the commissioner, losing his self-control.

Alwaar turned red. He felt he was responsible one way or another for what happened.

"We just don't have enough men," he said, embarrassed. "This is always the problem."

The chief scowled and walked around his desk until he faced the detective.

"From now on, I'll give the order to approve everything you request. I know it's too early to make judgments but I also know you'll do your best. I trust and rely on you."

Alwaar bowed his head respectfully and went back to his office at the end of the hallway. He looked over at Boukrisha's empty chair and checked his watch. The detective only felt at ease at the station when Boukrisha was there. It was nine o'clock and there wasn't any trace of his partner yet.

The detective thought the first thing he had to do was look for Othman. If he'd really run away, that'd be definitive proof of his guilt. Alwaar lit his third cigarette of the morning and started flipping through his notebook slowly. He read his notes carefully and took down the names of the people he needed to question. This crime is progressing in the way that pleases every criminal detective, he thought to himself. Once you've got a prime suspect, you don't need to look far.

The sound of footsteps clacking on the hallway ground pulled him out of it.

A middle-aged foreign man entered the detective's office. He was wearing an expensive suit that made him look like a diplomat. The features of his face were restrained and he had an air of dignity.

Alwaar stood up quickly, putting out his cigarette and hiding the ashtray in his drawer.

"Bonjour. Are you Monsieur Alwaar?" the man asked in a very refined tone.

The detective extended his hand and greeted the visitor while looking at him closely.

"Yes. Please sit down."

"Thank you. I'm Monsieur Michel Bernard, from the French Cultural Center. I received a phone call yesterday from Othman Latlabi, the husband of our friend Madame Sofia Beaumarché. He told me she was murdered."

Alwaar scrutinized Bernard's face. Despite all the smoke lingering in the office, he could smell the scent of his visitor's fine cologne.

"It regrets us to inform you this is indeed true," said Alwaar, making use of everything in his dictionary of politesse. "We were with Othman when he called you. We were expecting your visit."

"I wanted to come sooner," said Bernard, shaking his head in grief, "but the news came as a heavy blow to my wife. It was not possible to leave her alone."

"Does the victim have relatives here in Casablanca?" Alwaar ventured, moving his hand in a tired motion.

"No. She had a single son who lives in Paris. He spent a short vacation here and left a week ago. I informed him about what happened. He might arrive in Morocco today."

"And Othman?" asked the detective flatly. "Did you see him this morning?"

"I telephoned him at home but no one responded. I also called his cell phone but it was turned off. Do you have any idea who the killer is?"

"Until now, no."

"If you please, I would like to hear from you details of what happened."

Patiently and deliberately, Alwaar recounted the basics, arranging the events in his particular way. He kept waiting for Bernard to comment on them, but the visitor remained calm and composed.

"Strange," said Bernard finally. "According to what you say, theft was not a motive."

"Do you know if she had any enemies?" asked the detective.

"Sofia was dear to everyone," Bernard replied decisively. "She was blessed with a charming personality. Wherever she was, she spread joy and happiness."

"Please, Monsieur Bernard, I'd like you to tell me more about her personality. Othman said you were a close friend."

Bernard crossed his legs and relaxed a bit in his chair. His eyes filled with gentleness, as if he were immersed in happy memories.

"We were friends from the day she moved to Morocco. We were more like family."

"What was her profession before coming to Morocco?"

"She was a teacher of French literature. Her first husband, Monsieur Robert Beaumarché, was a banker. He died in a car accident. . . ."

"Othman told us that after the death of her French husband, she married a Moroccan," said Alwaar, cutting him off.

"Oh, Majid," Bernard blurted out. "Their marriage lasted about ten years. She met him in France."

"What was the reason for their divorce?"

"It's no use recounting the details," said Bernard, shaking his head disdainfully. "I was one of those who intervened to solve the problem. I can assure you it ended in complete understanding."

Alwaar remembered what Othman said the day before about this problem but kept going.

"Her first Moroccan husband," the detective asked with a hint of restraint, "was younger than her too?"

"This was Sofia's weak spot, her love for young men," said Bernard, letting out a small comforting laugh. "Of course, she had opportunities. After her husband Robert died, she received a large payout from his life insurance policy, in addition to the portion from the crash itself."

"Why'd she decide to live here in Casablanca?"

"She always had a taste for Morocco. It's a country of sun and vacation, she used to say. But her husband Majid was the one who convinced her to open the restaurant and live here for good."

"And Othman?" asked Alwaar slowly.

"I don't know how he found her. But if you want my opinion, he's a well-educated and very kind young man. He has a law degree from the French track."

This information had a heavy impact on Alwaar.

"So he married Sofia for the money?" he asked, smiling.

This question didn't surprise Bernard.

"It's obvious. Othman was unemployed when he married her."

"Do you have any idea about how they ran their financial affairs?"

"From what I know," said Bernard with a smile, "there weren't any disagreements between them."

"And the estate?"

"On that point, you'll have to check with Monsieur Shafiq Sahili, their accountant. He's in charge of all of Sofia's property and documents."

Alwaar opened his notebook.

"Shafiq Sahili. His address, please?"

"Abd al-Mumin Boulevard, number sixteen."

After this, Alwaar didn't ask a single question. He sat frozen, surprised that the number was sixteen. It was the number of his favorite horse, the one he'd dreamed about stumbling out of the gate. Was it a bad sign? Alwaar decided not to bet on the horses this week. He'd buy some lotto tickets instead.

6

BOUKRISHA DIDN'T HAVE ANY TROUBLE finding the address. Because of all the time he'd had to spend in the poor neighborhoods of Casablanca, Derb al-Fouqaraa was like an open book between his hands. He'd been there more than a few times to deal with one problem or another.

Boukrisha had four men with him. They left the police car far from the area, just to make sure no one saw them coming. One inspector took his position at the entrance of the neighborhood and another was pinned next to the main electricity posts. As for Boukrisha, he went straight for Othman's parents' house together with Asila. Despite how quickly they moved, the Derb's residents knew perfectly well something was up.

Boukrisha knocked on the door with several successive raps. He didn't wait long before the door opened and Othman's father appeared.

"Police," said Boukrisha with his repulsively hoarse voice.

"Please come in," said the father quickly, afraid of the neighbors crowding around.

The two inspectors walked into the house without saying a word. Boukrisha looked around the rooms and the kitchen. He tried to push open the bathroom door and realized it was locked.

"Who's here?" he said rudely, turning abruptly to the father.

"My wife."

"So you're Othman's father?" said Boukrisha roughly, giving the man a menacing look.

He nodded.

"Where is he?"

"He was here but he left."

"Where'd he go?"

"To the police station."

Boukrisha exchanged a glance with Asila, who seemed distracted and worn out from lack of sleep. Alwaar had punished Asila for falling asleep on the job by giving him an extra shift.

Othman's mother came out of the bathroom.

"My son's innocent, sir," she said immediately. "He's innocent!"

Boukrisha ignored her and turned to the father.

"He told you what happened to his wife?" he asked sternly.

"Yes," replied Othman's father. "We're very sorry for her."

"When'd your son come here?"

"Around six o'clock."

"If you've got any doubts about my son, you're wrong," said the mother, butting in. "He couldn't kill a fly."

"Shut your mouth!" Boukrisha screamed at her, quickly becoming enraged. "Don't open it unless I tell you."

The father's face went pale and the mother was so shocked that she scurried over to the nearest chair and sat down, putting her head between her hands.

"Listen to me closely," Boukrisha let out, threatening the father. "I'm going to call the station right now. If your son isn't there, I'll know you're lying. And I'll take you out of here in handcuffs."

He pulled out his cell phone and dialed Alwaar's number. After a few quick words, Boukrisha's eyes burned with anger. He put his cell back in his pocket, took out his handcuffs, and waved them in the father's face.

"Othman's not at the station," he said angrily. "Where'd he go?"

The father backed up to protect himself from the inspector.

"I didn't lie to you. I swear to God!"

"Maybe he hasn't gotten there yet," the mother chimed in. "You know there's a lot of traffic."

"Shut your mouth, you!" shouted Asila, suddenly coming to life.

She covered her eyes, feeling like she was on the verge of passing out. Boukrisha began pacing around the room and then headed toward the father, waving the handcuffs in front of him.

"You're hiding information from the police. That's enough to arrest you."

He started to put the cuffs on him, but the father took a step backwards shaking. He suddenly tripped on the hem of his jalbab and fell to the ground.

"A man at your age, lying!" Boukrisha yelled in his face, leaning over him. "If your son isn't at the station by noon, I'll come back here and arrest you."

He gave the mother a contemptuous look and pointed at Asila to head out.

The neighbors had crowded around the door, trying to figure out what was going on. When Boukrisha walked out, he yelled at them to move, waving his handcuffs in front of him. They all darted off.

As soon as he got back to his car, Boukrisha called Alwaar, who told him to go to the restaurant next and see what he could find there.

They took off racing through the city streets at top speed, passing all the other cars. The three inspectors crowded together next to the driver. As for Asila, he was spread out on the back seat, dozing. When the car stopped in front of the restaurant, he opened his eyes but stayed still, pretending to be asleep. He smiled to himself as he heard Boukrisha talking to the others.

"Leave him. He's not worth a thing when he hasn't slept."

The restaurant's main door was shut. While Boukrisha banged on it with his fist, the other two went round to the back, where they found a small metal door that led directly to the kitchen. One of the inspectors rapped on it with his key ring and someone came quickly to open up. It was the chef, Abdelkader. He looked depressed and had traces of tears in his eyes. Behind him, the inspector saw other people craning their necks to see what was going on, as if the bang on the door had surprised them in the middle of a heated conversation.

"Police," said the inspector, walking into the kitchen with his partner right behind him. It didn't take long before Boukrisha joined the two.

The kitchen was clean and neat and smelled of ammonia. Boukrisha stared down Abdelkader with the severe look of a cop. He then turned to Suleiman and Nureddin, inspecting them with the same harsh stare. He finished, finally, with Rahma and then remembered she was the maid Asila told him about. Boukrisha noticed that her eyes, despite being bloodshot, were wide and beautiful.

"You're Rahma, right?" he asked, giving her a command-ing look.

She burst out crying.

"Yes, sir."

Boukrisha looked over at the others presumptively.

"She's the one Asila told about Sofia's murder?" he asked in a voice that was becoming increasingly hoarse because of all the yelling he was doing.

They all nodded.

"Who saw Othman this morning?" asked one of the inspectors.

They stayed silent. Boukrisha went near Rahma and shoved his face in hers, as if he was about to kiss her.

"You work at Sofia's villa too, right?"

She took a step back, scared and nauseated by the inspector's breath, which reeked of cigarettes.

"Yes, sir."

"We're deeply affected by what happened to Madame Sofia," said Abdelkader in a grief-filled tone. "She was a good person."

The inspector stared at him with a look that immediately reduced him to silence.

"When'd you usually go to her villa?" asked Boukrisha as he turned back to Rahma, resuming his interrogation.

"Every day at seven in the morning, except for Saturday and Sunday."

"What time would you stop?"

"Around noon. I'd start working here in the evening."

"Notice anything recently?"

It seemed she didn't get his question. Boukrisha kept pressing.

"A fight between Othman and Sofia? A squabble, something like that?"

"No, sir. I never saw them fight. They got along well."

"And yesterday? Anything happen?"

"No, sir."

"What'd you do yesterday when you were at the villa?"

"The usual housework. I started by cleaning the kitchen and making breakfast for Madame. I then cleaned the floors, dusted the furniture, put the dirty laundry in the washing machine, and cleaned the bathrooms."

"And Othman? Where was he?" Boukrisha asked abruptly.

"Sleeping. He usually gets up at about ten o'clock and goes out to the market."

"Did he go yesterday?"

"No, he woke up late, around eleven. He sat in the kitchen and asked me to make a glass of orange juice for him."

"Where was Sofia?"

"Outside doing some gardening. It's her favorite thing to do."

"Did you hear them talk about anything?"

Rahma drew in her breath, hesitating a bit to figure out what to say.

"I don't remember them talking much but Madame came into the kitchen and told him to hurry up because they were late for something."

"Where were they going?" asked Boukrisha, his eyes darting back and forth.

"I don't know. Madame told me to go away."

"Was she mad at him?"

"Maybe. She didn't call him chéri like she usually does."

"Did she tell you to leave earlier than usual?"

"No. It was around noon."

Boukrisha stood there and stared at Rahma until she lowered her eyes. Scowling, he left her and began pacing around the rest of the employees, holding his hands behind his back. He stopped in front of Abdelkader.

"What do you do here?"

"I'm head of the kitchen, sir."

"You got anything to say? Any trivial detail might be useful for us."

"What's going to happen to us now that Madame's gone?" asked Suleiman in a grieving voice, not giving Abdelkader the chance to reply.

"That's your problem," said one of the inspectors.

Boukrisha's cell phone rang in his pocket. He got the order to come back to the station immediately.

Boukrisha found Othman sitting in the office in front of Alwaar. He was hunched over in the chair as if he was trying to warm himself up. His legs began shaking nervously and his face was pale and sickly. His chapped lips quivered and a look of fear appeared in his eyes as Boukrisha started talking.

"The best thing you ever did was turn yourself in," he said.

"I wasn't on the run," said Othman disdainfully.

Boukrisha grabbed him by the collar and shook him violently.

"Don't you raise your voice at me, understand?" he screamed in Othman's face.

"Leave him alone," said Alwaar with a hint of mockery. "He has a law degree from the French track."

This information lit Boukrisha up, who didn't even have a college degree. His voice became sharper, as if he was feeling a bit of envy.

"Even a PhD in criminal justice won't help him with us," he said bitterly.

Alwaar winked at Boukrisha, indicating to him to calm down.

"So, let's start from the beginning," said Alwaar, flipping through his papers and addressing Othman with a deadly heaviness. "You said you left to take the dog out for a walk around eleven at night, as usual. When you got back, you found your wife murdered, right?"

Othman nodded.

"How'd you know she was dead?"

Othman's words got stuck in his throat. He felt like the noose was tightening around his neck. He remembered his fingerprints might be on the knife handle. He closed his eyes as if he was about to pass out. The detective and inspector exchanged glances, watching him closely.

And what if his prints aren't on the knife? He can't remember if he wiped them off or not. What he remembered clearly was washing off the blood that was stuck to his hands after calling the ambulance and the police. He decided not to risk telling the details of what happened until he knows if his prints are on the handle. There's no way they could've received the lab report yet, Othman thought to himself. He let out a sigh and shook his head trying to drum up some courage from inside.

"She was still and wasn't breathing," he said, his eyes not focusing on anything. "I thought she was dead."

Alwaar seemed like he wasn't listening to Othman. He flipped through his notebook and lingered for a while on a page.

"Did you meet anyone while you were out with the dog?" he asked without looking up.

This question led Othman to deduce the kind of investigation the detective was following. Othman loved police novels and had some solid knowledge about criminal investigations he picked up from law school. He knew the detective would get past the little details first and then go straight to what would let him get at evidence that'll prove the charge.

Othman thought about all the possible ways he could answer the question. He then decided to risk giving them Naeema's name, hoping to send the investigation in a different direction, which might eventually prove to be even more difficult for him. But, if nothing else, this would stop them from talking about the crime, at least for the time being.

"I've got an alibi for when I was out with the dog," he said, taking a deep breath as if getting rid of a heavy burden. "I wasn't alone. My girlfriend was with me."

Neither cop interrupted him. It was as though what he'd said wasn't anything new. Alwaar lit a cigarette, even though he didn't smoke during interrogations. He knew this information was worth the exception.

"Why didn't you say that yesterday?" asked Boukrisha, butting in.

"I didn't think things would go in this direction," said Othman in a naive voice.

He then asked if he could have a cigarette and Alwaar nodded. A cloud of smoke soon filled the office.

"What's the name of this girl?" asked Alwaar calmly.

"Naeema Lamalih."

Alwaar took the name down on a blank page in his notebook.

"Where does she live?"

"Al-Jabal al-Dhahabi Street, number five, Maarif."

Alwaar paused a moment at the number five. He realized it was the number of a jockey who loses the race all the time.

"Where and when'd you meet her?"

"Two years ago. She's a sports trainer at Yasmina Club. Actually, she was Sofia's trainer."

Boukrisha bit down on his lips. Parts of the puzzle were starting to fall into place.

"Your wife," Alwaar said without looking up from his notebook, "she worked out at Yasmina Club. Naeema, her trainer, she's your girlfriend, right?"

Othman nodded.

"How'd you two first meet?"

"By chance. I was waiting for Sofia outside the club. She came out with Naeema and Sofia introduced us."

Alwaar moved his head as if the rest of the story was obvious.

"How'd it happen you were with your girlfriend near the villa past eleven at night?"

Othman took a number of drags on his cigarette, one after the other, and then put it out in the ashtray in front of him on the desk.

"Actually, we meet near a square not far from the villa where the dog would play," he replied without the least hesitation. "We meet there almost every night. Naeema drives over and waits for me there. We chat in the car for fifteen minutes and then she leaves."

"Don't you meet at other times?"

"Almost never. Sofia's very jealous. She'd watch my every move. She rarely left me alone."

The detective smiled and put out his cigarette.

"How'd you pull off these nightly meetings with Naeema, so close to the villa?" Boukrisha asked, quickly lighting up a cigarette of his own.

"My pretext was taking the dog out for a walk. After a while, it seemed normal to her and she didn't ask any questions. She never thought I was meeting someone while out with the dog."

Alwaar kept quiet for a while, turning over a number of ideas in his mind. He leaned his head back and closed his notebook with a bewildered look in his eyes. It seemed like he was about to make a decisive call. Othman and Boukrisha locked eyes waiting for Alwaar to start talking.

"Don't leave the city," he said to Othman bluntly. "Wait for us to contact you."

Othman jumped up as if he'd just had an electric shock.

"That means. . . ."

"Goodbye."

A look of brash happiness appeared on Othman's face. He shook Alwaar's hand warmly but when he turned to Boukrisha, the inspector looked away. As Othman left the office, Boukrisha slammed the door behind him.

"You let him go just like that?" he asked, unable to hide the anger in his voice.

Alwaar got up, putting his hand on his lower back in fatigue.

"And what do you want me to do in this age of democracy and human rights?" he said derisively. "There's no more falaqa, no more shock treatment, no more beatings or torture. If I kept him here, we'd have to take him to the DA after forty-eight or seventy-two hours at the most. And what would I tell him? We don't have any proof against this guy. All we can do is keep him under surveillance twenty-four hours a day. And you're the one who's going to arrange it. I want a detailed report on his movements at the top of every hour. And I don't want to hear again he slipped away. Understood?"

7

DETECTIVE ALWAAR REACHED THE DOOR of the building
where Yasmina Club was located. He waited a few minutes
until he heard the sound of people coming down the stairs.
He then saw a group of women wearing jackets on top of their
workout clothes. They had just taken a shower.

He looked at his watch and saw it was seven in the
evening. He began pacing in front of the building door with
his hands in his pockets. He didn't have any idea what time
Naeema got off work. When he saw some other women go in
the building with sports bags, he was sure another aerobics
class was about to start. He decided to take advantage of the
break between workouts and headed in.

The bright neon lights scattered through the club glittered
along the wall mirrors. He heard some women's voices laughing gracefully. The scents of perfume mixed with sweat clung
to his nostrils. The ground was covered with yellow leather
exercise pads. There was a door leading to the locker room,
where the voices were coming from.

As for the workout area, it was empty except for two young
women lying on their backs. Alwaar felt embarrassed by their
tight spandex clothes that revealed the curves of their bodies.
He turned around quietly and went back out to the street.

The first woman was Naeema and the second, shorter one
was Selwa. No older than twenty-four, Selwa was extremely
attractive, with short hair dyed light blonde.

The two were lying down, relaxing and talking in what seemed like a whisper.

"The old lady's dead," said Naeema, looking up at the ceiling.

Selwa sat straight up and looked over at her friend.

"Dead? That's impossible. She was doing aerobics here yesterday with the best of 'em."

"She didn't die a natural death," said Naeema without moving. "She was murdered."

"Who killed her?" Selwa asked in a tone full of fear as she put her hand on her chest, staring at Naeema.

"God knows. Yesterday, I was with Othman at our usual place. When he went back to the villa, he found her murdered, with a knife stuck in her stomach."

Naeema noticed her friend's hands were shaking, and sat up.

"What are you thinking about?" Naeema asked, perplexed.

"If that's what really happened, God will keep you safe," said Selwa, smiling strangely.

A woman came into the workout area from the locker room. Naeema looked at her watch.

"Othman will have a lot of problems with the police before they find the killer," she said, getting up.

"Do they suspect him?" Selwa asked with a hint of fear in her voice, putting her hand over her heart.

"He went to the police station this morning and hasn't called me yet."

A group of women, most of them overweight mothers, came out of the locker room. They were wearing tight sports clothes that accentuated their stomachs, breasts, and backsides, which had grown flabby from sitting in front of their computer screens for too long. Most of them were bank and company employees. Apart from them, there was a group of single and recently married women who were still fit. These were the ones Sofia would insist on working out with.

Naeema yelled out for them to follow along with her. She looked for Selwa and saw she had disappeared.

Outside on the street, Alwaar finished his second cigarette and decided to storm that place of perfume and sweat. He scaled the stairs for the second time, panting. He walked to the door at the end of the hallway and without hesitation went in the club.

"What do you want?" yelled Naeema at him immediately. "Women only!"

The detective nodded, but that didn't stop him from looking closely at the face of this beautiful woman and at her perfectly round breasts.

"Are you Naeema?" he asked, struggling not to steal a glance at the others.

When she heard him utter her name, she knew immediately who he was. Her face went pale.

"Yes, I'm her."

"Criminal police. Can we talk a bit?"

She didn't want anyone to pay much attention to this visit. She turned around quickly and Alwaar took advantage of the opportunity to let his eyes wander over the women. It seemed he was enjoying the view so much that he didn't hear Naeema ask him to follow her.

"Please go ahead," she repeated in an embarrassed voice.

She led him to the next hallway, opened an office door, and asked him to go in. She left him alone for a minute and in no time, she came back wearing a light jacket over her sports clothes. She closed the door and stood opposite him. Alwaar noticed that her face was pale. He could almost hear the beating of her heart. He was waiting for her to say something, but she didn't break the silence.

"No doubt you know why I'm here," he said in a monotone. "You were expecting me."

She shook her head to throw her hair back from her face.

"No, I wasn't," she said, looking away from him. "But I know why you're here. Othman came over this morning and told me what happened. He then went to see you at the police station."

Alwaar nodded, pleased with what she said.

"What'd he tell you exactly?"

"He said he found his wife murdered."

"Didn't he tell you where he was when she was killed?"

She hesitated for a moment, remembering that Othman told her to tell the truth. Her face betrayed how nervous she was.

"He was with me. We've had a relationship for two years. We don't have a chance to meet, except late at night. We talk for about fifteen minutes in my car and then I leave."

Alwaar looked at her with a knowing smile on his lips. The door opened suddenly and a brown-skinned woman wearing cleaning clothes and holding a broom stepped in the room. She was shocked to see a man in the office.

"Naeema, they're asking for you outside," she let out in a rough voice.

Alwaar took out his business card and handed it to her.

"Tomorrow at ten o'clock. I'll be waiting for you at the station."

Naeema finished work at nine in the evening. She took a shower, got dressed, and wrapped her hair in a wool cap without much care. She went down the building stairs and walked quickly toward the gas station where she'd left her car. She was agitated and wanted to get back to her apartment as quickly as possible.

The street was empty except for some taxis speeding by. The trip back to her house seemed to take forever. Alone in her car, she felt overcome by fear. She kept checking her rear-view mirror and drove in the far right lane, trying to avoid the attention of busybody drivers. She was relieved when she got to the door of her building. As she was parking between two cars, the night guard came out like a ghost. He was about fifty years old. He wore a suit like a military uniform and had a thick stick in his hand. He greeted her with his head lowered and began waving enthusiastically for her to back up. The guard's presence made her feel safe. She opened her purse, took out ten dirhams, and gave the coins to him as a tip on top of the monthly sum she paid him.

After getting out of the car, she opened the door of the building with her key and went up the stairs two at a time with her athletic agility.

Once she was gone, the night guard walked down the street, looking furtively around him until he stopped at a car parked in the distance in a dark space.

"That's Naeema, his girlfriend," he told the driver quickly and then walked off.

There were two inspectors inside the car, one of them holding the police radio. He called the station to pass on the information since the inspectors didn't need anything else. They already got from the guard everything they wanted and more.

As she climbed the final flight of stairs to her door, Naeema suddenly put her hand on her chest, about to scream out in fear. She didn't expect to find Othman sitting outside her apartment waiting for her. She wasn't happy to see him submissively crouched on the ground with his head buried between his knees.

"Did any of the neighbors see you like this?" she grumbled, hurrying to open the door and get him inside.

She turned on the lights and shut the door, staring at him. He seemed like a stranger to her with his unshaven face, withered eyes, and distressed look. She dropped her purse on the couch and went straight into the kitchen. The small apartment had two rooms, an entranceway, kitchen, and bathroom. The furniture was neatly arranged and the place gave off an air of relaxation, proving its owner was a good decorator.

Before she met Othman, she shared the apartment with another woman who worked in one of the big companies in Casablanca. She made it hard for Naeema to meet Othman, so he suggested to her to ask the roommate to move out, offering to pay the whole rent, which was about Naeema's entire salary.

"Why didn't you call?" she asked, taking a bottle of water out of the refrigerator.

"I tried several times," he said in an angry tone, throwing himself down on a small chair. "Your phone wasn't on. Why didn't you call me?"

She held the bottle of water up and drank until it was empty.

"That's not important. What'd the police do with you?"

Othman felt she was overwhelmed by anxiety. She left him for a moment and came back after taking off her coat and cap. She shook her hair a number of times, spreading it out like silk, and then collected it in a ponytail. Othman swallowed with difficulty.

"They asked me about this and that and I kept telling them the story of what happened. I had to confess to them I was with you when I took the dog out for a walk."

She threw herself down on the chair opposite him.

"A detective came to see me at work. He asked me to go to the police station tomorrow."

She gave him the business card and Othman looked to make sure it was Alwaar's.

"What'd he ask you?"

"He wanted to double-check I was with you."

Othman's eyes widened.

"What'd you tell him?"

"The truth."

Othman nodded his head approvingly. She then stared at him with a doubtful look.

"Othman, you've got to be honest with me."

The question scared him.

"I swear to you, Naeema," he said in a low voice. "I did-n't kill her. You know we both wanted her gone. But if I was planning on killing her, I'd have taken every precaution. . . ."

"Who killed her then?" she asked, cutting him off sharply in a way he hadn't experienced before.

His eyes strayed and he felt weak. He found himself think-ing about the fingerprints.

"If you're afraid for yourself," he yelled out, agitated, "you can be sure I'll clear you of any charges. Even if they frame me for her murder, they'll be putting *me* to death, not you."

Despite this, her scowl didn't go away.

"Did you eat?" she asked, opening the fridge to see what was inside. "I normally only have cheese and fruit for dinner."

He took her firmly in his arms and gave her a long kiss on the mouth but she didn't react. Finally, she pushed him away.

"You reek of alcohol. How can you drink at a time like this?"

He threw himself down on the chair again.

"I left the police needing some time alone to think about what happened. I went into a bar and had one beer and then another. I was there all day. I couldn't go back to the villa or my parents' house. My father's reaction to the news was disgusting."

"What happened when you told them?"

"They cursed at me for marrying her. How quickly they forget all the help she gave them."

Naeema put some plates on the table.

"After that cop visited me tonight," she said, trying to hide her suspicions, "I'll tell you the truth. I started to get scared. When I think about tomorrow, I feel like I won't be able to sleep tonight. But what bothers me the most is that I feel you're hiding something from me."

"Don't you believe I didn't kill her?" asked Othman bitterly.

"I was angry when I left you at the park. I admit I acted harshly, so I'm afraid the way I treated you made you do something crazy."

He took her hand and squeezed it firmly.

"I didn't kill her, Naeema. What I told the police and what I'm telling you is the truth. But whenever I think about the real killer, I feel dizzy. I can't think of anyone who has a reason to kill Sofia but me. Because of how much I hated her and how often I imagined killing her, I feel like I'm the one who did it. Her death was exactly what we both wanted. But I didn't do it. You've got to believe me."

Naeema let out a deep sigh of relief and pressed down on his hand gently.

"Thank God," she said. "You didn't do anything crazy."

"I'm innocent, even if the whole world's against me," blurted out Othman.

They went into the bedroom, took off their clothes, and got under the covers. The soft light from the bedside lamp illuminated the room. Othman now had all the time he wanted and didn't have to make love quickly, like he used to when he'd rush home to Sofia full of dread. He breathed in the scent of youth emanating from his love's body. What a difference there was between her and the old lady who'd crumble in his arms like a bag of rotten potatoes. His soul was filled with disgust at his past life and he thought about how he'd spend this night without any kind of deception.

Even though they weren't talking about Sofia's death anymore, he couldn't stop himself from obsessing about the fingerprints. He lay in bed afterward, tossing and turning, unable to sleep.

"There's something weighing on me, Naeema," he said in a voice full of tension, letting out a sigh and pulling her to him forcefully. "I have to confess it to you, but I beg you, I beg you to keep trusting me. When I left you and went back to the villa, I didn't find Sofia dead. She was dying and pleading with me with her eyes to pull the knife from her stomach. I didn't have to, but I did it. The situation was stronger than me. I pulled out the knife and put it on the bed. I then rushed to the phone to call an ambulance and the police. I thought she was still alive and would tell me who attacked her. But she died a few seconds later. In all the confusion and agitation, I forgot to wipe my fingerprints from the knife handle. Or maybe I did. I just can't remember. And that's what terrifies me. If the police find my prints on the knife, that'll be hard evidence of my guilt and I'll face many problems, especially if the police haven't found the real killer yet."

He pressed his chest against hers.

"All I want from you, Naeema, is that you don't ever doubt my innocence. I didn't kill Sofia."

Her tears wet his chest. She didn't utter a single word.

It was ten thirty at night when the commissioner called in Detective Alwaar and Inspector Boukrisha urgently. He went over the latest developments in the case with them and read aloud the most important parts of the medical examiner's report, which he'd just been faxed.

"She received two deep stab wounds," he read, proceeding slowly with the key information, skipping through lines that weren't important. "The first was in the kidney and stomach, and the second pierced the heart deeply. There isn't any evidence of resistance on the part of the victim. . . ."

"That means she wasn't surprised when she saw the killer," Alwaar said, cutting him off. "He's someone she knows."

"Her husband," said Boukrisha, trying to make his voice less hoarse. His comment didn't garner the least bit of attention.

The commissioner continued reading the rest of the report and then put it down in front of him on the desk.

"From your report on the crime scene," he said, addressing the detective, "the furniture wasn't overturned and nothing was broken. There's not even any evidence the killer tried to flee the crime scene. It's as if the victim surrendered completely and the killer knew exactly what he was doing."

"What's the time of death?" Alwaar asked in his tired voice.

"About quarter after midnight," said the commissioner, scanning the report.

"And what about the lab report?" asked Alwaar, shaking his head.

The commissioner waved his hand in a way that revealed his annoyance.

"I don't know how they work at that lab," he said, losing his patience. "We still haven't gotten anything from them."

Boukrisha's cell phone rang in his pocket. He rushed to get up and scurry over to the farthest part of the office. He was afraid it was a personal call but he relaxed when he heard the voice of one of his inspectors assigned to watch Othman.

"Okay, all the lights are on?" he said, trying to raise his voice so the others could hear him. "Then he'll probably spend the night with her. No, don't move from your spot. Wait for my orders."

"The target's still at his girlfriend's," he told the commissioner directly, putting the cell phone back in his pocket. "Looks like he'll sleep there."

The commissioner leaned back in his chair, rubbing his fingers under his chin.

"Excellent, excellent," he said spontaneously. "I think our theory's solid: Othman's the killer and his girlfriend's an accomplice, if not in carrying out the crime then in planning it. She won't be of any use to him as an alibi since they were together near the villa at the time of the crime."

"Why don't we go arrest them right now on the charge of perversion and carrying on an illegal sexual relationship," blurted out Boukrisha. "That way, we can take our time grilling them about the murder."

The commissioner liked the idea and then looked over at the detective.

"What do you think?" he asked, double-checking with Alwaar.

"Why dirty our work with some marginal charge?" he said, after a moment of hesitation. "We'd look like we're bumbling around and reaching for evidence. One more day and our man will break down and start singing like a sparrow."

The chief laughed out loud, his white teeth flashing.

"You're right," he said gratefully, "especially since the French embassy and the press are following the case."

8

THE NEXT MORNING AROUND NINE o'clock, the commission-
er's office was full of people. Besides the commissioner and
Alwaar, Michel Bernard—an advisor at the French Cultural
Center—was there, together with Jacques.

"Let me introduce you to Sofia's son, Monsieur
Beaumarché," Bernard said in a tone full of grief. "He just got
in from Paris."

The commissioner shook his hand warmly and then
extended his condolences with all the feeling he could muster.
Alwaar and Boukrisha did the same thing. The commissioner asked them all to sit down and mumbled again some
expressions of consolation. Looking back and forth between
Alwaar and Boukrisha, he was talking in an official style as if
he was giving a television interview. Between one expression
and another, he repeated his regret for the painful incident.
He reassured the two visitors that the entire police force was
working day and night to arrest the killer.

Jacques played with the black sunglasses he was holding in
his hands.

"Excuse me for interrupting, but please, monsieur, do you
have a suspect?" he asked.

The commissioner exchanged a glance with the detective
as though consulting him. He seemed to hesitate. In matters
like this, there were a number of points crucial to the investigation that should not be revealed to the public.

"And you, Monsieur Beaumarché," said the detective to save the commissioner from answering the question, "do you suspect anyone?"

Jacques leaned forward a bit as if the question shook him from his grief. Alwaar seized the opportunity to look closely at him and was struck by his elegance: Jacques had on an expensive black suit, a silk tie, and well-polished black shoes. Traces of the tragedy were clear in his eyes, which were surrounded by black rings, and his face was pale. He was obviously exhausted from the trip to Casablanca.

"It's difficult to respond to your question," he said, stammering without moving his head. "I don't know exactly who my mother knew and who she did business with. I visit her once or twice a year at the most."

"He was here last week," Bernard cut in as if he wanted to protect Jacques from talking. His eyes were full of grief. "He spent a number of days with us. I still remember when we said goodbye to you at the airport, Jacques. Your poor mother was so active and full of life. Who could have expected that she would be murdered a few days later?"

Jacques's eyes welled up. He took a tissue out of his pocket and wiped his eyes with it.

"I want to see her," he said, struggling to control his grief.

"Yes, yes," said the commissioner getting up. "I'll accompany you myself."

Once they were outside, Bernard suggested they take his car, a new Mercedes with diplomatic plates. The commissioner got in next to Bernard and Jacques sat in the back for the trip to the morgue. Alwaar waved goodbye to them and then went over to his meager Fiat Uno. He found Boukrisha already in the driver's seat, waiting for him.

As they drove off, Alwaar told Boukrisha to avoid the main roads, which were full of traffic at this time of day. He then asked the inspector about the latest reports from the surveillance team.

"Naeema left the building at about eight thirty wearing a jalbab," Boukrisha replied, turning off onto a nearly empty side street. "She put a bag of trash in the dumpster. One of our men searched it and found fruit peels and a lot of cigarette butts," he continued, smiling at this unnecessary bit of detail. "She then went to the local bakery and bought two hilaliya. She also got a container of milk from the grocer and a pack of Marlboro Lights from the cigarette seller."

"Who's on surveillance today?"

"Assou and Khouribgui."

Alwaar looked at his watch and remembered that in an hour, he had to cook up that sports trainer over high heat. He stopped the car on Abd al-Mumin Boulevard, which was full of high-rise office buildings and bank and insurance company headquarters. The detective asked Boukrisha to wait for him in the car. He went to the door of the building, which had a number of square brass signs for doctors, lawyers, and engineers on both sides. The detective noticed a sign with the name of the accountant Shafiq Sahili written on it.

He took the elevator up and stepped out onto a dark hallway that was covered with red rugs. He took a deep breath and rang the bell. A girl with short hair dyed light blond opened the door for him. She was wearing clothes similar to those of a flight attendant and had on high heels. She gave him an exaggerated secretary's smile.

"Excuse me," said Alwaar. "I have an appointment with Shafiq Sahili."

"Please, monsieur, come in," she said in a welcoming tone.

She closed the door and asked him to sit down on an elegant leather couch.

"Who shall I say is here?"

"Detective Alwaar."

The accountant's office had a large reception area, which became silent for a moment after the secretary walked off.

Alwaar looked around the room and saw fine paintings on the walls. The secretary's office was luxurious, despite being quite small. She had a nice computer with a flat screen and a PDA. Alwaar had never seen Shafiq Sahili but he guessed that if he was a reckless man, he would've already rolled around on these red rugs with his beautiful secretary.

"Please go ahead," said the secretary, hurrying back to her office.

The accountant stood up as the detective walked in. Sahili was about forty-five and the hair above his temples was going gray. He had on fine gold-rimmed reading glasses. He gave the detective a full look, shook his hand, and asked him to sit down. He then sat back in his own chair.

Alwaar looked around the office and found that the reception area was much more plush. He gestured over toward the open door, and the accountant immediately understood what Alwaar was getting at.

"Selwa!" he yelled out.

With the detective's back to her, she stuck her head into the room and then closed the door quietly. Alwaar wondered if she was eavesdropping.

"You're entrusted with the estate of Madame Sofia Beaumarché?" asked the detective sluggishly.

The accountant sat back and stuck his lips out in relief, clearly expecting something else.

"Of course."

He continued watching him closely.

"Don't you know what happened to her?"

The accountant's eyes widened.

"No. What happened?"

Alwaar took a deep breath, taking his time as if he was about to let out a sneeze.

"She was killed in her home the day before yesterday."

The accountant took off his glasses and put them down in front of him on the desk. He leaned forward in disbelief.

"Killed or died?"

"She was stabbed to death in her bedroom."

The accountant put his head between his hands, as his face went pale.

"Who killed her?" he said before the detective could ask him another question.

"That's what we're trying to find out."

"Was she alone?"

"Yes."

"Was it thieves?"

The detective got annoyed with the accountant's questions.

"We didn't find any evidence of that," he said, clearly irritated. "Please, I've got some questions for you," he said as he took out his notebook. "When did Sofia become your client?"

"Years ago," the accountant replied absentmindedly.

"What kind of work did you do for her?"

The accountant shook his head, looking at the detective with disapproval of how quickly he was going. Alwaar remained firm, waiting for a reply.

"I'm responsible for her estate."

"What does it consist of?"

The accountant got up and opened a drawer in his filing cabinet. He flipped through a number of files and then pulled one out. He came back to his desk and opened it in front of the detective.

"There's the restaurant—Sofia's in Ain Diab—the villa in Anfa, and bank accounts in both dirhams and euros," said the accountant.

Alwaar wrote down the information. He took his time before raising his head from his notebook. The accountant noticed from the detective's eyes how interested he was.

"Is there a will or something like that?"

The accountant leaned back in his chair and thought for a while before answering.

"Yes, there's a will."

"When did she deposit it with you?"

They exchanged a long glance. From behind the door, Selwa's heart began pounding.

"That's confidential. I think talking about it requires some time."

Alwaar put his notebook and pen down on the desk. He put his hand in his jacket pocket, took out his police ID, and showed it to the accountant.

"The person before you is a judicial police detective who has been charged with investigating the murder of Sofia Beaumarché. I'm asking you to provide me with all the information I need."

"Okay, okay," said the accountant, his face going pale. "I want to help. Forgive me. I just can't believe what happened."

"Excuse me," said the detective, "but I've got to do my job."

The accountant flipped through the papers in the file as the detective picked up his notebook and pen.

"Sofia," said the accountant looking closely at a sheet of paper, "was my dear friend for years. As for the will, she set it about seven months ago."

"Who's the beneficiary?"

"Her husband, Othman Latlabi," he said after a brief hesitation, as if feeling guilty for letting out a secret.

"What did she leave him?" said the detective, trying to remain calm.

"Her entire estate: the restaurant, villa, and bank accounts."

"Didn't she leave anything to her son?" Alwaar asked, moving his head with a sense of satisfaction.

"I asked her this same question when she deposited the will with me. She said she already gave her son half her money right after the death of her first husband."

Alwaar took his time before asking the next question.

"And Othman Latlabi, did he know about the will?"

"No," replied the accountant in a firm voice. "She was extremely vigilant on that point."

Alwaar closed his notebook and paused for a moment, wondering if there was anything else worth asking Sahili about. He then got up with his customary sluggishness and shook the accountant's hand.

"Thank you for the information."

"Is there some connection between Sofia's murder and the will?" asked the accountant, confused.

"The investigation's still at the initial stages," said Alwaar.

Behind the door, Selwa jumped over to her office, her chest heaving. She sat down, pretending to be typing at her computer as Alwaar left the accountant's office, hoping he'd go straight out the door.

"Goodbye, Mademoiselle," she heard him say.

She lifted her head in a jerky motion and stood up nervously. She walked Alwaar to the door and opened it, mumbling something, wishing she could hide her face.

"Goodbye."

She closed the door as soon as Alwaar set foot outside.

He went over to his car, threw himself down into the passenger seat, and slapped Boukrisha on the back of his neck.

"Our man's still in the arms of his lover?" he asked in a speed he only needed once or twice a year.

"I haven't gotten any new reports. That means he's still there with her."

Alwaar looked at his watch and saw it was nine forty. He had to make a final call on Othman.

"In the name of God, the boat's anchor and course," he said, smiling and slapped Boukrisha on the nape again.

Boukrisha knew exactly what he meant by this expression from the Quran. The car set off once again with a rattle. Alwaar took out his cell phone and dialed a number.

"Who's this? Assou? Is the target still in place? Good. Wake up and go arrest him and his gazelle. We'll be there as soon as you get out of the building with him."

He flipped shut his cell and put it back in his pocket, looking out on the wide road.

"What's new?" asked Boukrisha, impatience eating him up.

"The victim," said Alwaar, as if he was giving a report, "willed her entire estate to Othman."

Boukrisha immediately looked away from the road and turned completely toward the detective.

"And there's the motive for murder."

"A golden motive," said Alwaar, laughing.

The car was doing fifty as they sped down Zerktouni Boulevard.

Naeema's cell phone rang. Othman was in the bathroom, while she was getting ready to go to the police station. She looked for her cell and found it on the table in the bedroom. Before getting the chance to say hello, she heard Selwa's voice, choked and whispering as if she was standing in a tunnel.

"Naeema, be careful, be careful! Don't give the cops my name. They know about your relationship with Othman. A detective was just here at the office and I listened from behind the door. He came asking about the will. Whatever you do, don't give them my name!"

"Where are you calling from?" Naeema shouted, her voice trembling with fear.

"From the office bathroom."

The call was suddenly cut off. Naeema stood there staring at the cell phone, not knowing what to do. Othman came out of the bathroom wearing shorts and a v-neck tee shirt that showed off his thick chest hair. He saw Naeema frozen in her spot in a state of shock.

"Who called?" he asked, expecting some bad news.

She tossed the cell on the bed and broke down in tears.

"We're in a trap, we're in a trap!"

He took her by the arms.

"Who called? What happened?" he yelled out forcefully.

"Selwa," she said, sobbing. "The police were just at her office."

Othman swallowed with difficulty.

"Do they suspect her?"

"Not yet, but she's afraid."

Othman's sense of helplessness doubled. He took her violently by the arm and sat her down on the bed, making her look him in the eye.

"Listen to me carefully," he said gently, trying to calm her down. "Once the police know I'm the beneficiary of the will, they'll think it's a good enough motive for committing the crime. But the will's confidential and until now, they don't know Selwa told us what's in it. Calm down and get a hold of yourself. When you're at the police station, whatever you do, don't give them Selwa's name."

He hurried to get dressed, trying to calm down. He looked over at Naeema on the bed. She was burying her head under the blankets, crying.

"You can't go to the station crying like that. Please, don't tell them anything about Selwa. If you do, they'll burn us both together."

She didn't lift her head from the blankets. Othman felt it was no use talking to her. He picked up his pack of cigarettes, went out the front door, and closed it gently behind him, as if he was trying to sneak out. Before he could head down the stairs, he heard the sounds of men moving quickly up toward Naeema's apartment. He didn't have any doubt it was the police.

He backed up quietly but instead of going into the apartment, he ran up the stairs, only stopping once he found himself on the roof. He spun around and, for a moment, the idea of jumping to his death was tempting. He then looked around in every direction and climbed a short wall separating the roof from the next building. He looked down as he went and was struck by vertigo. The street below seemed bottomless to him. He heard someone scream out nearby and saw a maid carrying a laundry basket staring at him in fear. He ran past her to the stairs. He almost tripped as he raced down them, three steps or more at a time.

He got down to the building door and pulled at it but it was locked. He turned to a narrow flight of stairs next to the concierge's apartment and went down them, not knowing where they'd lead. At the bottom, he found a small iron door, pulled it open and all of a sudden, he found himself in the building's garage. He looked over at the gate leading to the back alley and saw it was open. He ran to it like a sprinter with only a few feet to the finish line.

After the bell kept ringing, Naeema finally opened the door. She was extremely weak and didn't know Othman was gone. A crowd of police immediately pounced on her. If Inspector Assou hadn't grabbed her by the arms, she would've collapsed onto the ground. He held onto her longer than he should have, seizing the opportunity to have this soft, beautiful woman between his arms.

"Put her on the chair," barked Boukrisha, knowing what was on Assou's mind.

Alwaar came into the apartment with his deathly slowness and immediately knew Othman was gone. He shot the cops in charge of the surveillance a furious look. He then went over to Naeema, who was slouched on a chair in the kitchen. Alwaar asked for a glass of water, poured some of it on the palm of his hand, and splashed it in her face. She let out a sigh and her head fell forward toward her chest. Alwaar grabbed a chair and sat down in front of her. He gently lifted her head with his hand under her chin.

"Othman was here with you?" he asked in a calm voice, looking into her eyes.

She nodded.

Alwaar turned around, scanning the apartment.

"Where is he?" he asked, feigning surprise and holding her chin tenderly.

"He's not here?" she asked slowly.

"You didn't hear him leave?" The detective jumped up suddenly and screamed in the faces of his men. "Search the building and the surrounding streets. Everywhere!"

9

OTHMAN RAN THROUGH ALLEYWAYS FOR a long time, terrified he'd wind up back at Naeema's building. He was feeling like he wasn't heading anywhere in particular, but that he kept going round in circles. He only stopped after he found himself on Ibrahim al-Roudani Street, which was packed with people and cars. Cafés, businesses, and small stores lined both sides of the street. He slowed down and began collecting his thoughts, repeatedly turning around to see who was behind him. He kept hoping he was in another place, far from the eyes that were no doubt watching him. At every moment, he thought the police would pounce on him, throw him to the ground, and cuff him. Sometimes he imagined he was hearing voices calling out to him and the sound of feet running behind him.

He stopped on the edge of the sidewalk, waiting for a taxi. He felt his legs knocking together, barely able to hold him up. Suddenly, his stomach rumbled, announcing that he was going to have terrible diarrhea any minute. He was dripping with sweat and tried to move, but was frozen in place. For a few seconds, he forgot everything that had happened, but his heart skipped a beat when he saw an empty taxi. He waved at it wildly, almost leaping into the middle of the street. When it stopped, he pulled open the door and threw himself down on the back seat. Without the least thought, he told the driver to go to the city center.

He got out at the roundabout on Mohammed V Street, not stopping to take his change from the driver. He felt strange because he didn't have to go to the bathroom anymore. He walked up the street to a café that was dark inside. He went in and sat down at an empty table, hoping to get a hold of himself. He waved at the waiter and ordered an espresso. He noticed a guy walking around selling newspapers near the door and called him over. He bought four papers and looked up, trying to catch some light from the small bulb hanging from the ceiling. After the waiter came back, he started sipping his coffee without sugar, just as Sofia used to make it for him.

He told himself he had to stay calm. As his feelings of fear disappeared, a headache started taking their place. He pulled himself together and flipped through the first two papers without paying much attention, as if all he was looking for was news to fix the disaster he found himself in: something announcing Sofia wasn't really dead and that the crime didn't actually happen.

After his third cigarette, an idea came to him. He thought about leaving the city. But where could he go? He then thought about his family. The police would undoubtedly give them a taste of torture to make them confess where he disappeared. He remembered Naeema and his pain doubled. He felt in his pockets and realized he left his cell phone at her apartment. No doubt the cops had it now. Will she confess everything? Will she ensnare him in a trap? Naeema will cave, he thought. She'll pass out as soon as Alwaar stares at her with his horrible eyes and breathes his disgusting breath in her face.

Exhaustion came crashing down on him, and along with it a profound sense of loneliness. In positions like this, people need someone who understands them and will tell them to take it easy. He'd given up his last friend long ago. Sofia had driven him into isolation and separated him from everyone except her and her friends.

He became incredibly depressed and was struck by an intense desire for some kind of company. Should he write a letter explaining everything and commit suicide? This idea overwhelmed him to the point that he began to compose the letter in his mind. He smiled feebly and a light dizziness hit him. If he kept thinking like this, he'd go crazy. Thankfully, someone yelling out roused him from this insanity.

He picked up one of the newspapers and began skimming the headlines. On the second to last page, a picture of someone he knew made him pause. The man was about his age and had a serious look and a receding hairline that made him seem older than he was. Under the picture was the name Ahmed Hulumi. Othman was hit by a childish happiness. All of a sudden, he felt like himself again and could concentrate on what he was reading. He no longer felt emptiness.

He pored over the article and read it closely as if his salvation was somewhere in it. It was an article of protest in which Hulumi called for the government to speed up looking into files of political prisoners who had disappeared. He also wrote about forced arrests, for which the state authorities don't have any records, leaving their families searching for them for years. The seventies and eighties were a time when Morocco experienced political tyranny. The most horrific types of oppression were practiced, civil rights were con-fiscated, and many prisoners were killed, some buried in mass graves. Only now were people beginning to speak openly about that period.

With every paragraph he read, however, Othman felt more frustration. Was he thinking he'd find something about his case in particular? Hulumi was a student with him at law school. Othman remembered him well. Hulumi was thin and always wore the same clothes. A group of friends always crowded around him like they were his bodyguards. He had a stern personality and would ignite the flames of protest, addressing students for hours. He was a political activist who never felt hopelessness. Othman wasn't interested at the time in joining any group. Politics were never his thing.

How luck would smile on Hulumi. He became a lawyer at exactly the time when everyone thought he'd wind up at the bottom of a grave. For most people, it went beyond luck that Hulumi was still alive.

When Othman left the café, the sun was so bright he had to shut his eyes. He wished he had his sunglasses with him. He headed toward the nearest phone and dialed information a few times, but it was busy. On the sixth try, a hurried voice answered him with the phrase: "Maroc Télécom at your service." He gave her the name of the lawyer and asked her in the gentlest tone he could muster to search for the address. The woman told him with the same haste: "Mohammed V Street, number seven." The line suddenly went dead. He was only a few steps from Hulumi's office.

He had passed in front of Hulumi's building several times without ever noticing it, but he remembered having a couple of glasses of wine at the bar next door. The building had a wooden door with chipped paint. As Othman walked in, he saw that the walls of the stairwell were exposed and the stairs shook under his feet. It was a building from the colonial period and clearly needed some work.

Othman found the office on the second floor. The door was open. He hesitated and thought about backtracking, but closed his eyes and went in. He found himself in a narrow area with a window directly opposite another building. The place was totally silent. There was a door ajar and a dark hallway leading to the back of the office. He thought again about walking out.

All of a sudden, a door opened behind him and a woman in her forties wearing masculine clothes and no make-up came out. She smiled at him and asked what he wanted. Behind her, Othman saw shelves of files and leather-bound books. He smiled at her.

"Is this the office of Ahmed Hulumi?" he asked apologetically, as if he was in the wrong place.

She pointed at the end of the hallway with the pen between her fingers. Othman thanked her with a nod and walked down the shabby hall. He turned to his right and saw a bathroom. He heard the sound of water flowing monotonously. He shut his eyes, took a deep breath, and knocked on the door with the tips of his fingers.

"It's open," he heard a voice yell out. "Come in."

At that moment, he knew it was impossible to turn back. He turned the knob and pushed the door open. He didn't expect the lawyer to recognize him. Othman raised his hand in a gesture to say hello. The lawyer waited for Othman to introduce himself, but he stayed fixed in his spot beside the door, ready to bolt.

"Come in, come in," said the lawyer hesitatingly, as if he was in the middle of something.

There were a number of books and papers in a pile in front of him. The sun was coming in from the window that didn't have any shades. There was nothing on the walls. In a corner, a number of magazines and newspapers were heaped up in neglect.

The two men shook hands and the lawyer pointed to a worn chair for him to sit down.

"Maybe you don't remember me," said Othman. "We were students together at law school. You were in the Arabic track and I was in the French."

The lawyer sat up straight in his chair, clearly interested. Despite what Othman said, the lawyer couldn't remember a thing about their shared past.

"Do you also practice law?"

For a moment, Othman felt the lawyer was ridiculing him.

"No," he said restlessly. "I actually just read an article of yours in a newspaper. It was great."

A wide smile appeared on the lawyer's face. It was the kind of appreciation that filled him with delight.

"Thank you," said the lawyer. "We're trying hard to shift to second gear in building democracy here. But there are those who don't want to step on the gas too hard. And you, what do you do for work?"

Othman stared into the lawyer's eyes and the muscles in his face tightened. He thought for a moment about ending his visit at this point. The meeting wasn't going anywhere.

"I came to talk to you, to ask for your help," he blurted out like he was shedding a heavy burden. "The police are looking for me right now."

The lawyer got up, walked around his desk, and sat in the empty chair in front of Othman.

"What's the problem?"

"I'm accused of killing my wife. . . ."

"Did you do it?" asked the lawyer, cutting him off.

Othman trembled and a deep silence took over.

"No."

His face went pale like that of a corpse.

"You said the police are looking for you," said the lawyer, staring at him suspiciously. "Where were you before coming here?"

Othman thought the lawyer already had a poor opinion of him. He waved his hand and sighed.

"You've got to hear my story from the start so everything's clear."

He then began talking quickly as if he was afraid of wasting the lawyer's time. Othman told him about his years of unemployment and then how he heard about Sofia from her ex-husband and married her. At this point, he hesitated for a bit before revealing the age difference between them.

"She was more than forty years older than you?" said the lawyer, almost letting out a laugh. "So she's rich?"

"She has a fancy restaurant in Ain Diab, Sofia's. Maybe you know it? She also owns our villa in Anfa. Recently someone from the Gulf offered her four million for it but she refused. She also has huge bank accounts."

After he revealed everything about his wife's wealth, he talked about his life with her and their first three years together before he met Naeema. He confessed that after he met Naeema, he was so miserable he lived on the hope that Sofia would die. He said his feelings were in turmoil, and he finally realized that his youth had been ripped away from him.

The lawyer nodded and asked him to go on.

"Six or seven months ago," added Othman, "Naeema met a girl named Selwa, who signed up at Yasmina Club, where my girlfriend is an aerobics instructor and Sofia worked out. This girl, Selwa, is the secretary of the accountant Shafiq Sahili. The important thing is that Naeema became friends with Selwa. Selwa saw us together once and Naeema was forced to tell her about our relationship. At that point, Selwa told Naeema that Sofia went to Sahili and deposited a will with him. A week later, she revealed to Naeema the contents of the will and Naeema then told me everything."

"And what does this will stipulate?" asked the lawyer with great interest.

Othman sighed with grief.

"Sofia left me her entire estate."

The lawyer shuddered in his seat and looked at Othman suspiciously. He then asked him to continue.

"I won't hide from you," said Othman, "that after I found out the will stipulates I get everything, I got excited and the idea of killing her enticed me. But I'd kill her every day in my imagination only. Sometimes Naeema would tell me Sofia won't die until after we both got old. I got what she meant by that. But I also knew that whatever happened, I wouldn't ever be able to kill someone."

"I'm with you up to this point," said the lawyer. "When was your wife murdered?"

"The day before yesterday, in the middle of the night."

"Where?"

"At the villa, in the bedroom."

"What was the murder weapon?"

"A knife."

"And where were you when she was killed?"

"I was out taking the dog for a walk, as I did every night after I got back from the restaurant, around eleven o'clock. Naeema was waiting for me in her car near a square not far from the villa. While the dog ran around, we sat talking. Sofia was always sick with jealousy. She'd keep an eye on everything I did just to make sure I wasn't cheating. In fact, I suspect she sent people to spy on me, especially Abdelkader, the cook at the restaurant. The one way I could meet Naeema was when I took the dog out."

"You didn't meet her anywhere else?"

"I'd do everything I could to go to her apartment, but it'd always be a lot of work to pull off."

"Fine, let's go back to the crime. What happened exactly that night?"

"I left Naeema not as well as I could have. Time after time, she'd tell me how frustrated she was with our situation. She left furious that night, saying she was fed up, and I went back to the villa with the dog. When I went up to the bedroom, I found Sofia lying on the bed, covered in blood with a knife stuck in her stomach. She hadn't died yet. I ran over to her terrified and asked her what happened. She couldn't say anything but begged me with her eyes to pull the knife out. Trust me, that night, I forgot how much I hated her. All I wanted was that she'd stay alive, so I pulled the knife out and ran to the phone to call the ambulance. I also called the police. I told myself I had to be quick since she was about to die. At that moment, my first thought was that thieves did it. But nothing was stolen. All her jewels were still there."

"Okay. Go on."

"That's everything. She took her last breath a few seconds before the ambulance got there and after that, things get all mixed up for me. The house was full of cops."

"Who's the detective in charge of the case?"

"Someone they call Alwaar."

"Of course. He interrogated you?" the lawyer asked, annoyed.

"Yes, that night until dawn. They told me to go to the station the next morning but as soon as I got there, they accused me of trying to flee simply because I was late."

"Did they use any kind of violence to get a confession?"

"No, but I think they're convinced I'm the killer. I was surprised they let me go and told me to wait for them to call."

"Because they don't have any proof yet," said the lawyer. "It's in their interest for you to be free and to place you under surveillance. Go on."

"That's what happened," said Othman, clearly uncomfortable. "I spent last night with Naeema in her apartment and this morning, the phone rang and she was talking with Selwa who told Naeema the police went to the accountant's office. . . ."

"Do they know Selwa told you about the contents of the will?" interrupted the lawyer.

"No, I don't think so. Selwa warned Naeema on the phone not to mention her name, even if things get rough. Maybe the police visited the accountant as part of their investigation and when they found out I'm the sole beneficiary, it proved to them that I have a strong motive for killing my wife. They then came to Naeema's apartment to arrest me."

"This proves they were keeping you under surveillance," said the lawyer. "But you got away from them."

"Naeema was about to go to the station because Alwaar went to her work yesterday and told her to come by today. After she got Selwa's call, she broke down and started crying. I knew how serious the situation was and warned her not to mention Selwa's name. I left but before I went down the stairs, I heard footsteps coming up and I knew immediately it was the cops. Instead of heading down, I went up to the roof of the building, jumped to the next one, went down the stairs, and then left through the garage. I was wandering around and then sat down at a café to collect myself and read the papers. That's when I saw your picture and the article you wrote. And that's how I got the idea of coming here."

The room became silent.

"The real problem, in my opinion," said Othman all of a sudden in a terrified voice, "is the fingerprints."

"Do you mean your prints are on the knife?" asked the lawyer, surprised, looking closely at him.

"Maybe I wiped them off. Maybe not. That's what worries me. I never saw someone dying before and I was in shock. I couldn't refuse Sofia when she was begging me with her eyes to pull the knife out of her stomach. I didn't think she'd die. I also didn't think things would turn against me. That's why I didn't notice if I wiped my fingerprints off the handle. Maybe I did. I just can't remember."

"Honestly, I don't get you," said the lawyer, leaning his elbows on his knees. "You know you're the prime suspect in your wife's murder, but you spend the night at your lover's apartment. You remind me of Marcel in Camus's *The Stranger*. You've read it, right?"

"Yes," said Othman with a faint smile. "But Sofia's not my mother."

The lawyer liked the response.

"Let's cut to the chase," he said, as if giving a presentation in court. "You want me to help you and not treat you like the others. In this profession of mine, I don't always wait to hear the truth from my clients. But your problem's very serious. You've got to tell me the whole truth, complete and unedited. Did you kill your wife?"

"No, I didn't. You've got to trust me."

The lawyer went back to his chair and sat down. He stayed silent for longer than seemed necessary.

"When the cops have a prime suspect like you," he said finally, "there's no way they'll bother looking anywhere else.

There's a police saying that goes: 'Look for the one who benefits from the crime.' So for the sake of argument, if you're convicted of the crime, who's next in line for Sofia's estate?"

Othman mumbled some cryptic words and shook his head a number of times as if he didn't hear him clearly.

"Her son, Jacques," he said absentmindedly. "But Jacques couldn't be involved, first because he loves his mother and second because he was in Paris at the time of the murder."

"When was he here last?"

"A week ago. He spent a few days with us and left."

"Does he usually visit his mother this time of year?"

"No," replied Othman after thinking a little. "He usually spends August here. In the past few months, he started talking more and more with his mother on the phone, about once a week, and she'd call him sometimes too."

"When'd they start calling each other more?"

"Since she came back from France," said Othman, confused. "Seven or eight months ago."

"Do you think that has any connection with his visiting outside the month of August?"

"I don't know."

"She ever talk with her son when you were in the room?"

"Yeah. She'd pass on his greetings."

"You ever hear anything indicating a problem between them?"

"No, I don't think so."

"Why'd your wife go to France? Was there something pressing?"

"Actually," said Othman, "it wasn't normal for her to go at a time like that. We usually go together once a year and spend a week in Paris during New Year's."

The lawyer took a deep breath and paused for a moment to think.

"When'd you learn about the will from this Selwa?" he asked.

"Five or six months ago."

"You said your wife was in France seven or eight months ago, and you found out about the will after five or six. So it was after your wife got back?"

Othman swallowed several times nervously. He took out a cigarette, fiddled with it between his fingers, and didn't bother to light it. He was deeply immersed in thought.

"I think so. Yeah, afterward."

The lawyer hit his hand on the edge of the desk and got up.

"How well did you get to know this Selwa?" he asked, engrossed, pacing around the office.

"Not at all. I've never even seen her. Everything I know about her is from Naeema."

"And when did Naeema meet her?"

"After she joined the sports club."

"Hadn't she met her before?"

"No, I don't think so."

The lawyer kept pacing around the office.

"Did this girl ask for anything in return for telling Naeema the contents of the will?"

"No, nothing."

"That's strange."

The lawyer kept circling the room, absorbed in thought.

"This girl's a mystery," added the lawyer. "If it's true she only joined the sports club after Sofia set her will with the accountant, this means she got close to Naeema so she could tell her what was in the will. And Jacques, who told him in France what happened to his mother?"

"Michel Bernard, one of Sofia's dear friends. He's an advisor at the French Cultural Center."

The lawyer sat back down behind his desk.

"Tell me the addresses and phone numbers of all her close friends. And give me the accountant's too," he said, picking up a pen and piece of paper.

Othman gave him all the information.

"You've got to go and get a good meal," Hulumi said in a strict tone. "Then go to the police station and turn yourself in. Don't tell them anything about coming here. And watch out for Alwaar. He's part of the old school and thinks any deception's fair game."

"And if they find my fingerprints on the knife?" asked Othman anxiously.

"I won't discuss that with you now."

Othman got up after a moment's hesitation, as if he didn't want to leave. He threw himself suddenly across the desk and hugged Hulumi warmly.

"Trust me," he said in an affectionate tone. "I didn't kill my wife."

He left the office without waiting for the lawyer to reply.

10

IT WAS QUARTER PAST TWO when Othman got to the police station, which was almost empty since people don't get back from lunch until two thirty. Nonetheless, a uniformed policeman quickly called out to Othman, led him down the hallway, and told him to sit on a chair next to Alwaar's office. The cop went away for a moment and then came back, standing there as if pinned to the ground at the end of the hallway. It seemed he suspected Othman might change his mind and take off. Less than ten minutes had passed when Othman heard some noise and footsteps approaching. Alwaar and Boukrisha appeared with a group of about five men behind them.

Alwaar opened his office door, smiling at Othman and moving his head menacingly. He motioned with his hand for Othman to enter, and Boukrisha shut the door behind them. He took off his jacket and sat down in front of his typewriter.

"Let's wait a bit to ask where our friend was," Alwaar said to Boukrisha with his well-known heaviness.

Othman stayed on his feet since no one had asked him to sit down. Alwaar scrutinized him and noticed how different his demeanor was from the previous time. Othman was calm and displayed no visible fear, as if he wasn't feeling the terrible danger encircling him.

"Sit down, sit down," said Alwaar in a cautious voice.

Othman sat down in a relaxed way. The detective and inspector exchanged a glance.

"God gave you a chicken that lays golden eggs but you ruined it and you ruined yourself," said Boukrisha harshly. "Were you so afraid of everyone running from the sight of you with your wife? You're not even thirty-three and she was seventy-three."

"I'm innocent," said Othman confidently, "and I maintain my innocence."

Boukrisha let out a ringing laugh.

"Before you continue your lies," said Alwaar, "you should know the lab confirmed that your fingerprints are on the knife used to kill Sofia."

Othman was struck and his face went pale.

"Whatever the evidence against me," said Othman as soon as he regained his composure, "I'll maintain my innocence."

"In your case," said Alwaar, "whether you're innocent or guilty doesn't matter. The evidence is against you. Your fingerprints are on the murder weapon and the motive is obvious: to speed up taking over the estate that the victim had willed to you. You were at the murder scene when the crime took place. What's all this evidence lying about? You know the law and you know proof speaks for itself."

He stole a glance at his watch as if he had remembered something.

"And in a minute," he added, "I'll have a special surprise for you."

Othman shuddered and thought about Naeema. Did she fall in their trap? He heard a knock on the door. It opened and an inspector appeared with another person. Othman was stunned and his eyes widened as he saw the cook, Abdelkader, come into the room. Alwaar asked him to sit down. He took a seat in front of Othman, looking at him with hatred and total disgust.

"There is no power and no strength save in God," he said mournfully.

"When you called me," said Alwaar to Abdelkader, "you said you have something important to tell us."

Abdelkader shook his head with grief and looked away from Othman.

"You said Sofia was stabbed to death?" the cook asked.

"Yes, that's true," said Boukrisha.

"I discovered that the biggest knife we have at the restaurant is missing."

Without opening his mouth, Alwaar snapped his finger at Boukrisha, who got up, opened a drawer in an iron cabinet, and took out a file that he put in front of the detective. Alwaar flipped through a number of pages, pulled out a photo, and placed it in front of Abdelkader.

"Is this the knife?"

"Yes, that's it."

Alwaar gave the picture to Othman.

"Do you recognize this knife?" he asked.

Othman took a quick look at it.

"Yes, that's the biggest knife at the restaurant."

"When'd you take it?" asked Alwaar.

"I didn't take it," he said, his voice quivering.

"I know when he took it," said Abdelkader, glaring at Othman. "It was the night he committed the crime. We all left the restaurant together and before we drove off, I saw Othman get into the car next to Madame and turn the engine on, but he turned it off and ran back into the restaurant."

Othman was stunned and his face went pale again.

"Why'd you go back to the restaurant the night your wife was murdered?"

Othman couldn't open his mouth. He was frozen in his spot and his knees began shaking.

"I didn't go into the kitchen," he said finally with a bitter smile on his lips. "I went back to the box to take some money I forgot there."

"I don't know why you insist on lying," said Alwaar in a chiding tone. "You're a former student of the law and you know the legal code. All the evidence is against you and you're still defiant. Why all this nonsense? Is it only to torture us instead of us torturing you?"

Alwaar turned toward Abdelkader, thanked him, and told him to wait outside.

"I'm innocent of Sofia's murder," said Othman, about to break into tears. "I'm begging you to listen to me. If I was the killer, why would I leave my fingerprints on the murder weapon? Why wouldn't I wipe them off? Why'd I call the ambulance and the police as my wife was still dying in my arms? Why would I take the knife from the restaurant kitchen in front of a witness?"

"What do you want us to say?" asked Alwaar, cutting him off in a mocking tone. "Since you're asking these questions, you've got an answer for them. Whatever that may be, it won't change what the witness said against you. And it won't wipe your fingerprints off the knife. We've got all the evidence we need, whether you confess or not."

He turned away from Othman and ordered the inspector to start writing the arrest report.

11

THE LAWYER WOLFED DOWN A sandwich in his office and thought about the case for half an hour. He wasn't a hundred percent convinced of Othman's innocence but he wanted to proceed like any lawyer whose only job is to defend their client, regardless of whether they're guilty or not. He thought he had to do everything he could to help Othman, because even if he was guilty and confessed to the police, he might be able to get a conviction of murder without intent or premeditation.

The lawyer found himself wondering about the same questions Othman had asked Alwaar. Why would he kill his wife and then call an ambulance and the police? Why wouldn't he wipe his prints off instead of leaving them on the knife? He knew every suspicion would be cast on him because of the will, so why wouldn't he plan the crime with complete precision? It'd be crazy to get himself caught up like this intentionally to make the crime seem like some plot against him.

Hulumi kept turning ideas over in his mind. Since he didn't have all the facts about the case, he decided to start directly from the police saying that goes: 'Look for the one who benefits from the crime.' Besides Othman, who else could profit from Sofia's death?

He looked at the addresses and phone numbers Othman left him. He thought he should begin with Michel Bernard, the victim's dear friend. But if he introduced himself as

Othman's lawyer, Bernard would be on guard against him and wouldn't tell him anything. An idea hit him, and he picked up the phone and dialed a number.

"Hello? Monsieur Bernard?"

"Yes," replied a slow, dignified voice. "With whom am I speaking?"

"Let me express my sincerest condolences for what happened to Madame Sofia Beaumarché. I'm Monsieur Ahmed Hulumi, a lawyer and, at the same time, I assist on the legal page of the newspaper *al-Hawadith*, which wants to publish news on the case. We'd like to confirm some information if possible. You know very well there are those who want to exploit this horrible crime and give it another dimension that could harm our good relations with France."

Bernard was silent on the other end of the line.

"Do you prefer that I come visit you at the cultural center?" the lawyer continued. "Let's say in a half hour?"

"An hour's better."

"That's fine. Thank you."

Tharya Bouchama, the lawyer who worked in the other office, came back after a light lunch at the restaurant next door. She saw that her colleague's door was open, so she walked down the hallway and popped her head in.

"Tharya!" yelled out Hulumi. "Come here for a second."

She went into his office and sat down in front of him in a relaxed way. She glanced at what was left of his sandwich.

"Did you eat lunch here?"

"Yes. Listen, someone I used to study with hired me. He has a strange case."

"I saw him when he came in. He was hesitating and almost went back down the stairs."

Hulumi then told her about Othman's situation step by step. Tharya wasn't interested in cases like this. After her divorce, she took up cases dealing with women's rights and joined a number of women's organizations. Like her colleague, she published articles in the press. She defended women's rights and called for the modernization of the personal status laws.

"I want to investigate this case like a cop," continued Hulumi. "If I can prove Othman's innocent, I'll have enough evidence to show the law has to be changed so a lawyer can be present when the judicial police question a suspect. I can do that by writing a series of articles about this in the press. Democracy in Morocco has to begin from the police stations. Human rights don't mean a thing if people can't have a lawyer there to defend themselves against the police. Lawyers don't even know what their client said at the police station. He could've been tortured or asked for a bribe or forced to sign a forged police report. And what if he's illiterate like half the population of Morocco? The police can write whatever they want and make him sign a confession without even knowing what's on the paper. If we can't ensure the rights of the criminal, how can we ever guarantee the rights of the innocent?"

Tharya smiled.

"But from what I heard, you don't have enough information about the case. . . ."

"I won't focus my investigation on the events themselves," interrupted Hulumi. "Only the police have all the details. I'll go on the theory that the real criminal wanted to trap Othman so they could profit from Sofia's murder."

"Who inherits if Othman's found guilty?" she asked.

"The victim's son, Jacques Beaumarché. He's the legal heir if Othman's convicted of killing his wife."

Tharya nodded along with Hulumi.

"You know the accountant Shafiq Sahili?" he added.

"Yes, I've worked with him on a few cases."

Hulumi suddenly became interested. He leaned forward with his elbows on the desk.

"Then I have to ask for your help."

"What kind of help?" asked Tharya slowly as her eyes narrowed in annoyance.

"Like I told you, the police visited the accountant and got from him all the information about the will. I don't think Sahili knows his secretary revealed the contents of the will to Naeema, Othman's girlfriend. This secretary couldn't have done that only to gossip. What I want from you is to go to the accountant, confirm everything that's in the will, and find out when it was written."

"And what are you doing?" she asked, lowering her eyes.

"I have an appointment in less than half an hour with Michel Bernard, the victim's close friend," he said, glancing at his watch. "I called him and told him I was a lawyer helping on the legal page of *al-Hawadith*."

"Why'd you do that?" asked Tharya, surprised.

"A lawyer's got to act like an investigator if he wants to be successful in these kinds of cases," he said with a smile, getting up and rubbing his eyes.

Bernard met Hulumi at the door of his wide office, which was decorated with pictures of the great writers of France. He closed the door and indicated to Hulumi to sit down on a leather couch.

"Let me introduce you to Monsieur Jacques Beaumarché, Sofia's son."

Hulumi tried to hide his shock at this surprise. He shook Jacques's hand warmly and expressed his condolences. Bernard walked behind his desk and sat down on his large, comfortable chair. He took a sheet of paper in French out of one of his drawers and presented it to the lawyer.

"I did my best to edit the news for you. You're welcome to retouch it."

Hulumi scanned the lines on the sheet. The information was concise, siding with the police and wishing them luck in arresting the criminal as soon as possible. The lawyer sensed Bernard wanted to end the meeting quickly.

"No doubt, monsieur, the news of your mother's murder stunned you," said Hulumi, looking at Jacques with a great show of sympathy.

"Certainly," he replied, annoyed.

"You got the news when you were in France?"

"Yes," he said sharply.

The lawyer had to think quickly. If he asked another question, it'd be obvious he was fishing for information and that'd make them both suspicious. But if he acted like he knew some new facts, that might get them interested.

"Do you know the police arrested Othman?" he said naively.

The two men exchanged glances and the lawyer saw what looked like a faint smile on Jacques's face.

"When did they arrest him?" asked Jacques quickly.

"This morning," said the lawyer, blinking.

"Impossible, impossible!" said Bernard, hitting his hands on the desk, struck by the news. "Why Othman?"

"I heard from my friends at the police that he confessed to the crime," said the lawyer.

"But why did he kill her?" asked Bernard. "She loved him and was happy with him."

The lawyer feigned innocence.

"Between you and me," he said, as if revealing a secret, "he killed her together with his girlfriend, Naeema Lamalih."

Bernard got up and paced around the office.

"The bastard!" he said furiously. "What will he get from killing his benefactor?"

The lawyer looked over at Jacques and saw that his pupils were dilated. His desire for answers was enticing him.

"Don't you know Sofia left her entire estate to Othman?"

Bernard froze in shock, while Jacques remained calm, as if that didn't mean he was cut out of his mother's will. Bernard put his hand gently on Jacques's shoulder, trying to help him digest the news.

"But did he know about the will?" asked Jacques suddenly. It was the question Hulumi was hoping for.

"If he didn't, why'd he commit the crime?"

Hulumi got up suddenly.

"I beg your forgiveness for disturbing you. Thank you for the information and your time."

He left quickly, not bothering to shake hands with either man. At the door of the cultural center, he took out his cell phone and dialed Tharya's number.

"Hello, Tharya? Where are you?"

"In the car. I left the accountant's office two minutes ago."

"Wait for me where you are," he said hurriedly. "I'll be right there."

He took a taxi and got out ten minutes later at Abd al-Mumin Boulevard, a few steps from the building where the accountant's office was located. He saw Tharya's car parked at a distance and rushed over to it. She opened the door for him and he got in next to her.

"You're all worked up. Did you get something?" she asked.

"I found Jacques with Bernard. I've got a strong feeling he's involved in his mother's murder. What do you have?"

"Sahili told me about the police's visit this morning. He doesn't think there's any connection between Sofia's will and the crime. As far as he's concerned, only Sofia and God knew what was in that will."

"How naive!" said the lawyer. "And the date of the will, did you get that?"

"At first, he thought the matter was still secret but when I told him the contents of the will, the hair on his head stood on end!"

"You told him about Othman coming to visit me?" he asked anxiously.

"Of course not. I hinted at Alwaar and he thought I got my information from him so he read me the text of the will. It was written on April seventh of this year."

Hulumi counted the months to himself.

"Less than eight months ago," he said. "This confirms what Othman told me. Sofia wrote her will after she returned from her last visit to France. Selwa signed up at Yasmina Club around the same time."

"And what do you conclude from that?"

"That Selwa signed up at the club after Sofia wrote her will and not before."

Tharya bit her lips in confusion.

"Good," said the lawyer with his eyes on the entrance of the building. "What about this secretary, Selwa?"

"She's the one who greeted me. She's about twenty-four, but she's more elegant than someone her age. I noticed she was worried about something and got all quiet."

"That's because she knows the police questioned the accountant. She's afraid her name will get mixed up in the investigation."

"I think Sahili trusts her more than he should. He doesn't bother to close his office door when he meets with clients."

"So she heard everything that went on between you two?"

"That's for sure. I was annoyed at first but it's not my business to give orders in an office that's not mine."

"I want to watch this girl," said Hulumi, gently pressing on his colleague's shoulder and looking at his watch. "I don't think she'll leave the office before six thirty or seven."

"There she is, there she is!" Tharya yelled out, pointing at the door of the building.

"Put your head down!" said Hulumi, excited.

Selwa stood in the middle of the street. Hulumi looked closely at her and thought she was elegant and beautiful. She was wearing a dress that made her look like a majorette. She had the face of a doll and her short hair was dyed blonde. While she was looking for a taxi, she opened her purse and took out her cell phone. She dialed a number and a heated conversation ensued.

"You want to take the car?" asked Tharya.

"No, it's not necessary. I'll make sure she doesn't see you. Turn on the engine and get ready to trail the taxi. She wouldn't leave work at a time like this unless there's something really important. Maybe it's got to do with you visiting the accountant."

Selwa got into a taxi. There was heavy traffic, so she didn't notice she was being followed.

"With you making a big deal about lawyers being present at the police station during the preliminary investigation," said Tharya, driving close behind the taxi, "you'll make problems for us we don't need."

"Lawyers work like this in the U.S. and Europe, not only using their assistants, but also resorting to private detectives."

"But there aren't any private detectives in Morocco," said Tharya with a laugh.

"We'll make them legal too," said Hulumi confidently, "and that way we'll limit the current omnipotence of the judicial police."

The taxi emerged from the congestion and passed Zerktouni Boulevard before stopping at a light at an intersection. It turned finally onto a wide street running parallel to the Atlantic Ocean and sped up. Hulumi told his colleague to keep pace.

"They're doing about fifty in a thirty zone," she protested.

"Are you afraid of getting a ticket?" asked the lawyer, laughing. "Don't. Speed up, speed up. If we lose her, we'll lose everything."

It was obvious Selwa was heading for Ain Diab. The taxi slowed down when the traffic picked up around McDonald's.

It finally stopped in front of the Shore Hotel, one of the best hotels in Ain Diab. Selwa got out of the taxi and hurried inside. Tharya stopped the car some feet away.

"Why'd she leave work in the middle of the day to come here?" asked Hulumi in surprise.

His colleague didn't pay any attention. He asked her to wait for him, got out of the car, and walked over to the hotel. From the front door, he saw Selwa standing at the reception desk. He then saw her head toward the elevator. At that point, he went in, wandered around the magnificent lobby, and then walked over to the reception. The man working the desk was young and chic. He had an attractive smile and his hair was combed with great care.

"Oui, monsieur," he said gently in a welcoming tone.

The lawyer wasn't sure how to proceed.

"Please," he stammered, "who's the girl who was here just a minute ago and took the elevator?"

The smile disappeared from the man's face.

"What's the problem?" he asked sharply.

"I want to know who she's visiting," the lawyer said, almost whispering.

The deskman took a step back.

"Why are you asking?" he said nonchalantly.

Hulumi thought about saying he was a cop but was afraid the man would ask for ID. He then slowly took out a hundred dirham bill, looked to the left and right, and put it down in front of him.

"This is yours," said the lawyer. "Take it quickly."

A look of fear appeared in the deskman's eyes. He was about to protest but he took the bill with striking speed and slipped it under the register in front of him, pretending to be flipping through it. A wide smile appeared on his lips.

"She went up to the fourth floor."

"Whose room?"

"A French guy named Jacques Beaumarché."

The lawyer almost let out a gasp.

"Jacques Beaumarché? When did he check in?"

"Yesterday."

The deskman shook his head as if telling Hulumi to leave. The lawyer took a few steps back and stayed still for a moment, shocked by what he'd discovered. He took a long look around the lobby, which was completely empty. He then went quickly back to Tharya's car, opened the door, and threw himself down on the seat next to her, almost out of breath.

"What happened?" she asked, scared.

"She came to see Jacques, Sofia's son. She went up to his room."

Her jaw dropped and she slapped herself on the cheek.

"I need a camera. If only I could've taken a picture of the two of them together," groaned Hulumi.

"What's she doing now?" asked Tharya excitedly.

"I don't know. I admit I wasn't prepared for a shock like this."

"Did one of the hotel workers see her going up?"

"I asked the guy at the reception and he told me she went up to Jacques's room. That cost me a hundred dirhams."

"Then you've got a witness," said Tharya, satisfied.

Hulumi was still stunned by what he'd found out.

"This is like something out of a police novel," said Tharya. "Make sure that you don't start thinking you're Columbo," she added.

"What I want to know about this girl," he said, ignoring her jibes, "is whether she told Jacques what was in the will. I'll bet she's had a relationship with him for a while. Then this sudden visit now. She came right after I met with Jacques at the cultural center and after you went to see the accountant."

"If she's working for Jacques, why'd she leak the contents of the will to Othman?"

After a moment the lawyer started in his seat and turned toward Tharya.

"It's Jacques. I'm guessing he knew his mother set her will with the accountant, watched Selwa, and then got close to her. He might have started a relationship with her or seduced her by saying he'd take her to France or something. I don't know. After their relationship was solidified, he made her

114

look at the will and when he found out his mother left everything to Othman, he set his scheme in motion. He told Selwa to join Yasmina Club and get close to Naeema. He then told her to leak the contents of the will, knowing Naeema would tell Othman. Maybe Jacques was hoping that'd give Othman a good enough incentive to kill his wife."

"But wasn't Jacques in France when the crime happened?" asked Tharya, digesting her colleague's theory.

"It's easy to hire a killer."

"I don't think he'd go that far. He probably figured the police would question Selwa and she might confess she told the contents of the will to Naeema and Othman."

"But no one would think he has a relationship with her," said Hulumi. "That way, he'd remain far from any suspicion."

"Didn't he think when Naeema and Othman mentioned Selwa's name to the police, she'd break down and confess her relationship with him?" asked Tharya.

"It's crazy that things are going in this direction since the police have only worked to convict Othman, without checking other leads. Even if we suppose Selwa confessed she told the contents of the will to Othman, what's the worst she'd face? No doubt Jacques went over all the possibilities with her."

Their eyes clung to Selwa as she darted out of the hotel. She stood in the middle of the road waiting for a taxi.

"What do we do?" asked Tharya, starting the ignition. Hulumi stared at her with a confused look.

"I don't know."

"Do we follow her?"

Before Hulumi could answer, Selwa got into a taxi and took off. Hulumi hit the dashboard despondently and kept silent.

"Are you waiting for inspiration?" said Tharya with a smile.

"I'm convinced Jacques killed his mother," he said, coming out of it. "And I don't think he hired anyone to carry out the crime. It's impossible to share a secret like that with some-one else. That could easily mean getting caught or facing con-stant blackmail. And if he was stupid and hired someone, he'd definitely try to get rid of them as soon as possible."

"And he'd get rid of Selwa if she knows what he did or sus-pects him," Tharya said cautiously, letting out a soft whistle.

After a moment of silence, Tharya started laughing.

"I think we're going a bit too far in all this guesswork!"

Hulumi didn't laugh along.

"We're facing a very complicated crime of murder," he said gloomily, "and the police won't ever doubt anyone besides the suspect they have. There may be evidence against Othman even though he's innocent. And the real criminal's free, counting his money without any worry. If we stop now, he'll just keep going and Othman will get convicted."

"But," said Tharya, "your client didn't bring you anything to prove he's innocent. From what you said about this case, he might've even left his fingerprints on the murder weapon."

"Yet the case is still open," said Hulumi with the smile of someone who's run out of patience.

He was incapable of making any decision. He then pressed on Tharya's hand gently.

"I'm sorry if I've taken up a lot of your time," he said.

She turned on the engine again and looked over at the door of the hotel.

"This Jacques, do you need him anymore?"

"No. All I've wanted to do at this point is cast a shadow of doubt on him."

12

HULUMI WENT INTO THE COURT building, presented himself
to the public prosecutor's office as Othman's lawyer, took the
police report to the photocopier, and then sat down in a corner to read it. He only lifted his eyes off the report twice. The
first time was when he saw the statements of the cook
Abdelkader, who accused Othman of sneaking into the
kitchen and taking the knife the victim was killed with. The
second time, he looked up as all the muscles of his face
twitched. The police report stated the fingerprints of the
accused were the same as those found on the murder weapon.
The lawyer thought this case was the most difficult he'd faced
in his career and he began to feel it was hopeless. It didn't
help that he was only permitted to read the report just
moments prior to defending Othman before the investigative
judge. The only thing that encouraged him to continue was
the fact that Othman hadn't confessed to the crime.

A half hour later, the lawyer met Othman in the hallway
leading to the office of the investigative judge. He was hand-
cuffed and a uniformed policeman held him by the arm. The
lawyer smiled at him gently and noticed he was suffering from
exhaustion and sleep deprivation. Othman lowered his head,
clearly humiliated.

Despite the simplicity of the office, it gave the impression
of gravity. The judge was a short man, about fifty-five years
old. He had a face with severe features and dark sunken eyes.

He was entirely bald and his lips were tight, making him constantly flash his teeth. He was famous among lawyers for his severity. Some of them thought he was a stubborn opponent but no one would deny his boldness in taking initiatives that flew in the face of formalities for the sake of speeding up the settling of justice and getting to the heart of a case.

As for the judge's secretary, she was a heavy-set woman about the same age wearing an elegant jalbab that matched the scarves covering half her head. She was a master of her work and knew what she had to write down and what she could leave out to the point that the judge never gave her any directions. Sometimes he'd forget she was even there.

The judge ordered the police to uncuff Othman and then pointed at a seat and told him to sit down. He waited until the policeman closed the door and then took out his reading glasses, which looked like those financial accountants wear. He put them on the bridge of his nose and flipped through the police report.

"Why have you not confessed your crime to the judicial police?" he said to Othman in a commanding tone.

Othman cast a glance at the lawyer appealing for help. Hulumi was sitting in front of him watching and waiting.

"I'm innocent, your honor," Othman stammered.

"All the evidence's against you," said the judge, turning the pages of the police report.

He turned away from Othman and looked at the lawyer, prompting him to speak.

"So, Ustaz, what do you have to say?"

Hulumi smiled and leaned forward so the judge could hear him.

"Yes, your honor," he said, "the evidence is indeed against my client but he hasn't confessed to this crime. If you please, my client has a degree in the law and was a colleague of mine at law school. Before going to the police, he visited my office and told me the details of what happened. I convinced him to face the counsel of the court. I then undertook some investigations and, if you please, I request that you summon the following people."

The lawyer opened his briefcase and took out a sheet of paper, which he presented to the judge. He read the contents of the paper in a loud voice.

"Jacques Beaumarché, the Shore Hotel, Ain Diab."

The judge turned his lips slowly without raising his head from the sheet.

"Who's this Jacques Beaumarché?"

"The victim's son."

The judge rested his chin on the palm of his hand and leaned forward.

"This request of yours will produce something new for the case?"

"Yes, your honor."

The judge turned his lips another time and continued reading.

"Selwa Laghyathi, 16 Abd al-Mumin Boulevard, Maarif."

"Who's this Selwa?" asked the judge, blinking his eyes.

"The secretary of the accountant with whom the victim deposited her will."

The judge suddenly seemed interested. Without raising his head, he read the final name.

"Jilali Bouchra, the Shore Hotel, Ain Diab."

"Who's this person?"

"An employee at the hotel who's in charge of the reception."

Othman bit his lips and looked at the lawyer and the judge. He felt himself forgotten in the session, despite the fact that he was the most important person in it. The judge took his time reading the sheet.

"I don't want to subject these people to useless trouble," he said without looking up from the paper. "Are you sure their presence could change something in the course of the case?"

"Yes, your honor," said the lawyer, sure of himself. "If you please, I ask your honor to summon them as soon as possible."

"Tomorrow at two o'clock," said the judge in a severe voice as he pressed his foot on the bell under the desk, suddenly ending the session.

The next day, after a delay of half an hour, the lawyer sat down in front of the judge. The latter was busy looking for something in his drawers and after five minutes of searching, he gave up. The lawyer was afraid this frustration might influence the judge's mood.

"Maybe what you're looking for is hiding because I'm here," he said, trying to lighten things up.

The judge cracked a smile, but his frown did not entirely disappear.

"Working in government offices grates on my nerves," he said, sitting upright in his chair. "Never mind. All the people I summoned are waiting. Should I call them in together or one at a time?"

"If you please, your honor, I ask you to call Jacques Beaumarché."

The judge pressed on the bell with his foot. There were knocks on the door and then the doorman appeared.

"Jacques Beaumarché," the secretary instructed him.

A minute later, a voice came from behind the door and the knob turned. Jacques came in. He stared at the lawyer, unable to hide his surprise. The judge shuffled forward on his seat and shook Jacques's hand.

"This is Ahmed Hulumi, the lawyer of the accused," he said, pointing over at him. "Please, sit down."

"We've already met," mumbled the lawyer.

Jacques sat down. He was elegantly dressed, as usual, but traces of insomnia were clear in his bloodshot eyes. The lawyer thought it was obvious that being summoned to the court scared him.

"Go ahead," said the judge, pointing at the lawyer.

"As you know, Monsieur Beaumarché," said the lawyer, addressing Jacques, "Othman, the husband of your mother—and we are very sorry for what happened to her—is the primary defendant in her murder. The presumed motive for committing the crime is the will your mother wrote that excludes you from the inheritance, while Othman, according to the will, is the sole beneficiary of her entire estate."

Jacques face became tight.

"Monsieur Beaumarché, did you have knowledge of this will before your mother's death?" asked the lawyer.

A stunned look appeared in Jacques's eyes.

"No, I didn't," said Jacques, hesitating. "But it doesn't bother me that my mother left everything to her husband. She was very kind to me and after she got Papa's life insurance years ago, even though she was the sole beneficiary, she gave me half the payout. My mother wasn't being unfair to me in any way when she willed her estate to her husband."

"Fine," said Hulumi. "Then you didn't know about the will?"

"I told you, no," replied Jacques, clearly annoyed.

The lawyer turned toward the judge.

"I have another opinion. You knew about the will your mother set with the accountant Shafiq Sahili. His secretary, Selwa Laghyathi, leaked its contents to you," he said, pointing at Jacques.

Jacques's face went pale. He seemed to be in a state of shock. The lawyer exchanged a glance with the judge.

"Monsieur Beaumarché," said the judge, trying to hurry a reply.

"I don't know what this man's getting at," said Jacques, addressing the judge bluntly.

"Do you know this secretary?" the judge asked Jacques in a commanding voice, looking over at the lawyer. "Answer yes or no."

"No," said Jacques in a decisive voice.

"Please, your honor, I'd like to call Selwa Laghyathi," said the lawyer, addressing the judge.

A minute later, the doorman brought her in and closed the door. Selwa was wearing a jalbab and had a scarf on her head. Her clothes made her seem older than she was and hid her usual attractiveness. She stood frozen in her place, looking at the men in surprise. The judge asked her to sit down.

"You're Selwa Laghyathi, the secretary of the accountant, Shafiq Sahili?" asked the lawyer as she threw herself down on the chair nervously.

She nodded, rubbing her fingers together.

"Do you know this man?" the lawyer added, pointing at Jacques.

She barely gave him a sideways glance and then shook her head.

"Look closely at him," said the lawyer insistently.

"I looked at him and I don't know him," uttered Selwa, the words leaving her throat with an uneven hoarseness.

"Fine," said the lawyer, folding his hands. "Two days ago, you left the accountant's office at four o'clock in the afternoon anxious and hurried. You took a taxi with license plate number 2230 and went to Ain Diab—to the Shore Hotel, to be exact. You asked the permission of the man at the reception desk and then went up to room number ninety-six to see this man," he said, pointing at Jacques.

Selwa's face immediately turned the same pale yellow of her dyed hair. The investigative judge noticed that Jacques gave her quick affectionate looks. The judge told the lawyer to move on and ask for the third person.

The young man who was in charge of the reception at the Shore Hotel came in and stood confused in the middle of the office, looking around at those who were there. He was wearing his work clothes, which looked like the suits worn by admirals. He was clearly nervous. All he wanted, when he was asked to talk, was to say he was innocent of anything that might be tied to him.

The judge told him to sit down on a chair in the far corner of the office.

"We won't take more than five minutes of your time," said the lawyer, smiling to lighten the deskman's nervousness as he sat down. "When I visited you at the hotel, what did I ask you?"

The chair shook under the weight of the young man. Immediately, the lawyer knew he was afraid the hundred dirhams he gave him would come out. The lawyer signaled furtively for him to hurry up and answer.

"You asked me about this girl," he stammered, pointing at Selwa. "She got to the hotel just before you. This man here," he said, pointing at Jacques, "told me if someone named Selwa asks for him, I should tell her to go up to his room."

"Do you still deny, monsieur," said the lawyer, addressing Jacques, "that you don't know this girl?"

Agitation got the better of Jacques.

"Great," he said angrily. "If I knew I was going to be interrogated like this, I would've also brought a lawyer with me."

"You have the right to hire a lawyer to defend yourself," said the judge with a firm tone.

"Is there a charge against me?" yelled Jacques in the judge's face, suddenly becoming excited.

"Why did you deny knowing this girl?" asked the judge sharply, angered by Jacques's rudeness. "And why did she go up to your hotel room?"

"This is a personal matter. I don't have to respond to that."

"This isn't a personal matter," said the lawyer. "It's connected to the will since this girl is the secretary of your mother's accountant."

"I object to all these questions!" yelled Jacques, stamping his foot on the ground. "I refuse to be interrogated until I have my lawyer."

"Don't talk unless I tell you to," said the judge with a calmness that increased with Jacques's anger.

"Do you still need this person?" he asked the lawyer, looking over at the deskman.

The lawyer signaled to the young man and smiled at him graciously.

"I'm finished with him, your honor," he said.

"Wait outside until I call you," said the judge.

The young man hurried out of the room and the doorman closed the door behind him.

"When did you join Yasmina Club?" Hulumi asked Selwa, catching her off guard.

She kept rubbing her fingers together and gave Jacques a quick look.

"I don't remember. Maybe a year ago or more."

The lawyer took his notebook out of his pocket and flipped through it quickly.

"It was six months ago," he said. "The club's records prove this. And you quickly became friends with Naeema. You knew about her relationship with Othman and you knew Othman was the husband of Sofia, who also worked out at the same club. You told Naeema you were Shafiq Sahili's secretary and revealed to her the contents of the will, isn't that right?"

Selwa lowered her head, thinking Naeema had confessed to the police that she was the one who leaked the contents of the will. She looked up and then stared off into the empty space of the room.

"I admit I did the wrong thing," she said in a low voice. "But it was Naeema who kept insisting when she found out I was the secretary of Sofia's accountant."

"Who told her that?"

"I don't know," said Selwa, staring out at nothing.

"Did you tell her the contents of the will?" asked the judge sharply.

She nodded. The judge was surprised, since this information wasn't in the police report.

"Does your employer let you look over all the confidential documents in his office?" asked the judge severely.

"I've never done anything like that before," she said in a bewildered voice. "But Naeema seduced me. She showered me with gifts and kept pestering me until I finally gave in. I had no idea doing that would make Othman kill his wife. . . ."

"Who told you Othman killed his wife?" interrupted the lawyer sharply.

Her face went pale and she swallowed with difficulty. She gave Jacques a pleading look and saw he was even paler than her. Her head shook forcefully and signs of indignation and hesitation appeared on her face. The judge saw how much she was suffering and gave her a piercing look.

"If you don't want to ensnare yourself even deeper, you have to be frank and recount the events exactly as they happened," he said. "Don't forget we're dealing with the crime of murder, which the law punishes with either life in prison or death."

Her teeth chattered as she remembered all the executions she'd seen in the movies. All of a sudden, she burst out crying.

"I don't have anything to do with Sofia's murder!" she yelled out in a choked voice.

"Who told you Othman killed her?" asked the lawyer.

"Him," she said suddenly in a clear voice, pointing right at Jacques.

"Did you visit him at the hotel?"

"Yes."

"Liar!" yelled out Jacques, hitting his knee.

The judge told him to keep calm.

"Is he the one who told you to leak the contents of the will to Naeema?" continued the lawyer.

Without hesitation, she nodded.

The judge sat back in his chair staring at Jacques.

"When did you tell Monsieur Beaumarché the contents of the will?" asked the lawyer quickly, trying to take advantage of her breakdown.

She continued crying. She didn't have any tissues with her so she wiped her tears on the sleeve of her jalbab.

"How did you meet this man?" asked the judge, taking the reins and pointing at Jacques.

"On the street, randomly," she replied, as if she wanted to end this ordeal as quickly as possible. "He told me I was beautiful and that it was love at first sight. I soon fell head over heels for him. After a couple of days, our relationship took off and he promised he'd marry me, saying he'd take me to France with him and give me a job in his company. He soon started to ask about my work and about the kind of clients the office works with. He then asked me who our foreign clients were and I mentioned Sofia to him."

"Didn't you know she was his mother?" asked the judge.

"No, your honor. He was surprised. He told me Sofia was his mother and then told me about her personality and about her marriage to a man more than forty years younger than her. He said this man is Othman and that he has a lover whose name is Naeema."

"When did he ask you to look at the will?" asked the judge.

"A few weeks after we started dating. He was stunned when he found out his mother left everything to her husband. He cried between my arms and said what hurt him wasn't being excluded from the inheritance but that a cheating husband would enjoy his mother's fortune. I told him to tell his mother about her husband's infidelity but he refused."

"Why?" asked the lawyer.

"He said he didn't want to cause her pain, especially since she'd just found out she had breast cancer."

Both the lawyer and the judge looked over at Jacques, who bowed his head in grief. Selwa continued rubbing her fingers. The judge told her to continue.

"He told me his mother, after her last visit to France, had a complete medical examination. The doctors discovered the beginning stages of breast cancer but she hid the news from everyone. He found out about it by chance when he saw her medical file sitting out and flipped through it."

"That's why he hurried up and carried out his plan," said the lawyer enthusiastically.

The judge gave him a cold look and then asked Selwa to go on.

"He told me to sign up at Yasmina Club," she said, rubbing her fingers again. "And to get close to Naeema and become friends with her."

"Is he the one who told you to reveal the contents of the will to her?"

She nodded.

"Did he say why?"

"I didn't ask. I was blindly in love with him and did what he told me to without asking questions."

She broke out crying.

"It's clear now, your honor," said the lawyer, taking advantage of the opportunity, "that the victim found out she had cancer during her last visit to France and immediately after her return, she set her will. It's also clear that her son was spying on her and what we heard now from this woman shows what Monsieur Beaumarché had in mind to make sure Othman didn't inherit his mother's estate."

"I excuse myself from any comment on these absurdities," said Jacques as calmly as he could with a bitter smile. "Yes, it's true I had a relationship with this girl and it's true I loved her and was intending to marry her. I pushed her to look over my mother's will since I was greatly pained by Othman's infidelity. I found out about his cheating by accident and it caused me great pain that my mother would leave her fortune to a man stabbing her in the back. As Selwa said, I didn't want to tell my mother about her husband's betrayal because I didn't want to see her miserable and alone. I also didn't want to be the cause of that pain. I never told Selwa to tell Naeema about the will. I know now there's a conspiracy against me."

Fatigue appeared in the judge's eyes. He took down some notes in the register in front of him.

"Your honor," said the lawyer, "I have proof this man wasn't in Paris at the time of the murder, as he claims. He was here in Casablanca."

Jacques shuddered in his chair and his face turned pale. His fingers trembled and he quickly hid his hands in his pockets. A smile of victory appeared on the lawyer's lips. As for Selwa, she still seemed confused.

"I visited Monsieur Michel Bernard," added the lawyer confidently, "the advisor at French Cultural Center who was a dear friend of the victim and also of Monsieur Beaumarché. As you know, your honor, the police report does not indicate in any way who told Jacques about his mother's murder and the reason is clear. The judicial police believed my client was the killer. When Othman visited me before turning himself in, I asked about this point and he told me Bernard was the one who informed Jacques in Paris. This morning, I visited Monsieur Bernard and he told me he tried to contact Jacques immediately after he heard the horrible news but no one responded to his call. As Bernard said, it was very late. He therefore sent an email to Jacques and the next morning, Jacques called and said he'll take the next flight to Morocco. And here you see, your honor, Monsieur Beaumarché only responded after he got the email, not before. When Bernard told me he met Jacques at the airport immediately after his arrival from Paris, I almost gave up on this theory. But I asked Bernard if he actually saw Jacques walk through customs. And here I was surprised by what he said. Jacques didn't tell Bernard when he was leaving Paris. Instead, he called him after he arrived at Mohammed V Airport, and Bernard found him outside, in front of the main entrance. Since this point was so important to my case, I went to the airport just to make sure. I talked with the chief of security and gave him Monsieur Beaumarché's name and passport number, which I took from the deskman at the hotel. I asked the chief of security for the list of travelers coming from Europe on the day Jacques claims he arrived in Morocco."

Hulumi took a folded up sheet of paper out of his pocket and handed it to the judge.

"Here's the list. You can see for yourself Monsieur Beaumarché's name isn't there. The reason is that he wasn't in Paris at the time of the crime. He was here in Casablanca."

Jacques got up as if he was about to flee. In no time, though, he collapsed back into the chair and buried his face between his hands.

Selwa fidgeted in her chair as she stared at Hulumi in surprise. A thick silence hung over the room. Jacques finally lifted his head and stared at the lawyer with a strange look of surprise mixed with hatred. His jaw jutted forward and a look of defeat and resignation appeared in his eyes. His frazzled appearance clashed with the natural politeness that was obvious from how he spoke.

"Othman's innocent," he said clearly without the least hesitation. "And this girl wasn't involved," he said, pointing at Selwa. "She didn't know anything about it. No, I didn't go back to France when I visited my mother the last time. I acted like I went through customs at the airport but I gave my spot to a pregnant woman and snuck out. My mother, Othman, and Michel thought they saw me off and that I took my plane. I knew for a long time about Othman's relationship with Naeema. I won't hide from you how much it pained me and how much it made me hate my mother's behavior even more. It was humiliating that she acted like a child and married two men much younger than her. But the will was the breaking point. It's unjust that my mother cuts me out and leaves her entire estate to a man stabbing her in the back. That fortune is mine. It has to be mine. It's my right."

He swallowed with difficulty.

"That night," he went on, "I snuck into the restaurant's kitchen after everyone left since I had a copy of the keys, but I was surprised when Othman came back. If he'd come into the kitchen, he'd have found me hiding there behind the door with the knife in my hand. I imitated a cat's meow and all of a sudden he turned around and walked out. Of course, I knew he met his girlfriend every night when he took the dog out for a walk. I waited until he went to see her and opened the door of the villa with my key. . . ."

He wasn't able to continue.

"You stabbed your mother with the knife you took from the restaurant's kitchen," said the judge.

He bent his head.

"It was bad luck for my client that he pulled the knife out of the victim's stomach," added the lawyer. "He left his fingerprints on it. How naive!"

"I'm the one who's naive," said Jacques with a faded smile. "I carried out what he'd dreamed of and gave him a life of security with his girlfriend."

13

IN ORDER TO CELEBRATE WITH his guests, Othman took the unusual step of turning off the outside neon sign that read "Sofia's Restaurant."

At the dinner table there was Detective Alwaar, Inspector Boukrisha, the lawyer Ahmed Hulumi, and his colleague Tharya Bouchama. Othman refused to join them until he finished counting up the receipts. He was sitting relaxed on his stiff chair behind the glass counter. All of a sudden he felt a light touch on the nape of his neck. For a second, he thought it was Sofia. He turned around impatiently and saw a magnificently beautiful woman whose stomach was round as a balloon. She had on a fantastic dress. Her hair was charmingly straightened as if she had just come from the hairdresser.

"Naeema," he said with a smile of joy on his lips.

He took her by the hand and massaged her stomach tenderly. He looked up at the picture of Sofia hanging on the wall inside a golden frame and let out a sigh. His eyes flashed with gratitude.

Around the table, the conversation was raging between Hulumi and Alwaar.

"What'll be left of the judicial police," said Alwaar, "if you and your lawyer friends stick your noses in our work?"

"Imagine," said the lawyer, "what would've happened if Othman didn't visit me before turning himself in to you, if I didn't tail Selwa and discover her relationship with Jacques. Don't forget that's what changed the course of the case and I discovered it before the police report was written, before Othman was turned over to the DA. It's a matter of lawyers in this country being there with the judicial police to defend their client. How many innocent people are abandoned behind bars because of shoddy police work? Without any doubt, Othman would've been one of them."

Alwaar lit a cigarette.

"I bet a lot of money using all the numbers that showed up in this case," he said with his well-known sluggishness, "and I lost. If you want, monsieur lawyer of the future, you and I could make a bet. I gave you all the police reports for the articles you published in the press. There's something in my report that proves Othman's innocent. If you hadn't put together the pieces of the case, I'd have come up with the same result. What is it?"

"Everything in your report," said the lawyer, "was against Othman."

"Are we betting?" asked Alwaar sharply. "Five hundred dirhams and I'll solve the puzzle for you."

"Don't let the police steal your victory," said Tharya to Hulumi.

"I say your report didn't have anything supporting my client," said the lawyer, perplexed.

"If this is your final word," said Alwaar, "then you lost the bet."

Alwaar called Othman over and made room next to him. He put his hand gently on Othman's shoulder as he sat down.

"I want to ask you a question," he said, clearing his voice of any kind of sluggishness. "And you've got to give me a straight answer. When you got back after the crime took place, you found a picture next to the bed where your wife was murdered. It was a picture of her with her son, Jacques."

Alwaar turned toward the lawyer.

"And this is in my report, right?" he added.

The lawyer nodded in agreement.

"Tell us, Othman, about the way this picture fell on the ground," said Alwaar.

A light fear appeared in Othman's eyes. He found it hard to return to the details of that awful night.

"Sofia was dying," he said finally, swallowing with difficulty. "She tried to speak but she couldn't. She turned to the picture and tried to pull it to her but she knocked it off the table."

"Sofia wasn't trying to pull the picture toward her," said Alwaar with determination, staring at Hulumi. "She was pointing to her son as the killer."

Hulumi let out a ringing laugh.

"You wouldn't have noticed that, Alwaar, if Othman was convicted," said Hulumi. "You're interested in it only because he was proven innocent. Sorry, you lost the bet!"

Translator's Afterword

THE PREHISTORY OF THE MOROCCAN Arabic police novel lies in the 1970s and 1980s, a period of grave human rights violations known as the Years of Lead. During this time, the Moroccan police and security forces arrested and tortured thousands of dissidents, many of whom are still missing and presumed dead. Synonymous with cruelty, capriciousness, and corruption, the police of 1970s and 1980s Morocco were widely feared and hated. Even uttering the word 'police' in public during the Years of Lead was considered taboo. It should therefore come as no surprise that the police almost never appeared in Moroccan works of fiction during those decades. Writing about or depicting the police at the time would have been a dangerous act with likely dire consequences.

All of this changed during the 1990s. A dormant economy, coupled with international pressure to improve the country's record on human rights and freedom of speech, compelled the palace to institute democratic reforms and launch a period of widespread liberalization. These initiatives also created a new atmosphere of relaxed restrictions on social life and public expression, leading more and more Moroccan newspapers to report on taboo subjects, including, most prominently, crime and police activities.

This growing liberalization produced new forms of fiction in Morocco as well. In the mid- to late 1990s, genres such as illegal immigration and prison literature began to appear.

While several prison novels had been published in the 1970s and 1980s and immediately confiscated, the late 1990s witnessed the first readily available and widely read accounts of the brutality Moroccans faced during the Years of Lead. The mass publication of books and newspaper articles openly depicting past human rights abuses soon led to widespread optimism about the possibility of substantial reforms in police procedure and respect for the rights of the individual. These hopes were further fueled by the feverish optimism that accompanied the arrival of the new king, Mohammed VI, in 1999.

It was during the heady times of mid-1990s Morocco that the first modern Arabic police novel was born. This new form of writing directly engages hard-hitting issues such as crime, human rights, and state authority, providing a powerful medium for social critique. In *The Final Bet*, originally published in 2001, Abdelilah Hamdouchi continues this literary experiment by engaging the themes of police reform and legal rights through the fictional story of Othman, a young Moroccan accused of murdering his much older wife. Because all the case evidence seemingly points to Othman, the brutal and outmoded cops in the novel make no effort to investigate other leads in the case. As such, the novel is a powerful condemnation of a police force incapable of adapting to the new age of respect for civil and legal rights ushered in by the end of the Years of Lead.

Moreover, the novel strongly criticizes how an individual arrested in Morocco cannot have a lawyer present during initial police questioning. In a 2001 interview with the Moroccan daily *al-Sabah*, Hamdouchi claims: "We know that at this delicate stage, when there's a specific crime, the fate of the accused—who is naked without defense—is decided. Because of possible disregards of the law, aberrations, or just plain ignorance, the police can easily ensnare someone in a crime they're innocent of." Left to the shoddy detective work of today's Moroccan police, the novel suggests, Othman would have been convicted for a crime he did not commit.

A key innovation in *The Final Bet* is the appearance of a lawyer who conducts an investigation on behalf of his client. For Abdelilah Hamdouchi, the image of the lawyer in the novel is not simply a condemnation of the police. It also serves as a model for reform of the Moroccan legal system as it concerns the rights of the individual. In the same interview, Hamdouchi explains: "Maybe by chance the appearance of *The Final Bet* will create what is at the moment a hypothetical character—that of the lawyer who has the right to be present with the police at the same time things really happen in a case. If lawyers in Morocco can be there from the beginning of the arrest, we might be able to avoid many of the pitfalls the police fall into." Even though all the case evidence points to Othman, the novel makes it clear that it must be the police—and not the hypothetical lawyer—who uncover the truth. In the *al-Sabah* interview, Hamdouchi explains the title of the novel as follows: "I mean by '*The Final Bet*' the bet that Morocco now faces—a bet on democracy, human rights, and establishing a state of law." Democracy, however, cannot be measured by words or freedom of expression. As Hamdouchi told me in a Rabat café: "The true test of democracy is in the police stations and not in the dome of parliament."

As a writer of police novels, Hamdouchi has dared to do what was not possible before: to enter the police station in order to show not only its inner workings in a realistic and critical way, but also to demonstrate the pressing need to reform the legal rights of the individual at the initial stage of a criminal investigation. Without his lawyer, Othman would have become the victim of a brutal, violent, and incompetent police force that shows little interest in adapting to the demands of the new Morocco. Without a full reform of the police, the novel suggests, there must at least be reform in the legal system that prohibits a lawyer from being present during the first forty-eight to seventy-two hours of a suspect's arrest. For Hamdouchi—and his lawyer in the novel—if the rights of the individual are not respected at the police station, all talk of democracy in Morocco is meaningless.

SELECTED HOOPOE TITLES

Whitefly
by Abdelilah Hamdouchi, translated by Jonathan Smolin

The Televangelist
by Ibrahim Essa, translated by Jonathan Wright

A Rare Blue Bird Flies with Me
by Youssef Fadel, translated by Jonathan Smolin

∗

hoopoe is an imprint for engaged, open-minded readers hungry for outstanding fiction that challenges headlines, re-imagines histories, and celebrates original storytelling. Through elegant paperback and digital editions, **hoopoe** champions bold, contemporary writers from across the Middle East alongside some of the finest, groundbreaking authors of earlier generations.

At hoopoefiction.com, curious and adventurous readers from around the world will find new writing, interviews, and criticism from our authors, translators, and editors.

THE FRIGHT AT ZOMBIE FARM

written by
Laurie S. Sutton

illustrated by
Scott Neely

THE MYSTERY INC. GANG!

SCOOBY-DOO

SKILLS: Loyal; super snout
BIO: This happy-go-lucky hound avoids
scary situations at all costs, but he'll do
anything for a Scooby Snack!

SHAGGY ROGERS

SKILLS: Lucky; healthy appetite
BIO: This laid-back dude would rather
look for grub than search for clues,
but he usually finds both!

FRED JONES, JR

SKILLS: Athletic; charming
BIO: The leader and oldest member
of the gang. He's a good sport – and
good at sport, too!

DAPHNE BLAKE

SKILLS: Brains; beauty
BIO: As a sixteen-year-old fashion queen,
Daphne solves her mysteries in style.

VELMA DINKLEY

SKILLS: Clever; highly intelligent
BIO: Although she's the youngest member
of Mystery Inc., Velma's an old pro at
catching crooks.

A famous artist has disappeared, and now zombies run wild on his farm! Only YOU can help the Mystery Inc. gang solve this case of zombies on the loose.

Follow the directions at the bottom of each page. The choices YOU make will change the outcome of the story. When you have finished one path, go back and read the others for more Scooby-Doo adventures!

YOU CHOOSE the path to solve the mystery of...

The crime-solving friends of Mystery Incorporated drive down a twisting country road, but they aren't on a case. They've been invited away for a weekend at a famous farmhouse.

"It sure was nice of our friend David Bush to ask us to come out to Bushytail Farm," Daphne says. "He's thinking of turning it into a boutique hotel."

"I can't wait to see the real Bushytail Farm. David has painted so many pictures of it, I feel like I already know the place," Velma says as she looks at an art book about the landscape paintings of Bushytail Farm.

Turn the page.

"You could say he's made a cottage industry out of it," Fred jokes as he drives the Mystery Machine.

The van passes a fairground. Delicious aromas float in the air. Suddenly Scooby-Doo and Shaggy pop up from the back of the Mystery Machine!

"Whoa! Like, I smell hotdogs!" Shaggy says and smacks his lips.

"Rand pie!" Scooby slobbers.

"How about some Scooby Snacks instead? We're almost at the farm," Daphne says as she shakes a box of the savoury treats.

"Rokay!" Scooby and Shaggy say as Daphne tosses a couple of treats towards the friends. **CHOMP!** The two gobble down the Scooby Snacks.

"Look! There's the entrance to Bushytail Farm. Just like in the paintings," Velma says. She points to a gate made of stone and iron.

Fred turns the Mystery Machine down the road leading to the gate. The road changes from smooth to rough. The van passes the old iron gates covered in rust and moss.

"Wait. This doesn't look like the paintings," Velma says, disappointed. "It looks … unkept. Are you on the right road, Fred?"

"I'm following the directions David gave me," Fred replies.

"Rit rooks haunted," Scooby shivers.

"Like, maybe we should go to the fair instead," Shaggy suggests. A picture of pies and cakes appears before his eyes.

"Too late. We're here," Fred announces.

The Mystery Machine stops in front of a farmhouse that looks like a sneeze could make it collapse.

The Mystery Inc. gang climbs out of the van. The charming cottage in the famous paintings is really a dirty dump!

Turn the page.

"That's not how David painted it," Velma moans.

"Maybe he was using his artistic imagination," Daphne decides. "It sure isn't how I imagined it."

"Like, the place is a wreck!" Shaggy blurts. Scooby-Doo whimpers in agreement.

"Rit really rooks haunted," Scoobs says and hugs his pal Shaggy.

WHAM! The gang jumps when something hits the side of the Mystery Machine.

"Go away!" an old man shouts at them. His fist makes a dent in the side of the van.

"But we were invited!" Daphne protests.

"David Bush asked us to come here," Velma adds. "Where is he?"

"Don't know. I'm just the caretaker. Nobody tells me anything," the creepy old man replies. He turns and shuffles towards the barn. The gang is so surprised that no one notices him talking into a small microphone.

"Like, what are we going to do now?" Shaggy asks his friends.

"I have a plan!" Fred announces. "Let's split up and find David. He'll explain everything."

"He has a lot of explaining to do," Velma states as she grimaces at the sad image of her fantasy farmhouse. "Something is seriously wrong with this picture."

"Velma and I will look for David in the house," Daphne says.

"I'll search the barn," Fred volunteers.

"He might be at the fair. Scoobs and I will look there," Shaggy says as his stomach growls.

To follow Shaggy & Scooby, turn to page 12.

To follow Daphne & Velma, turn to page 14.

To follow Fred, turn to page 16.

Shaggy and Scooby-Doo leave the rest of Mystery Inc. at Bushytail Farm and walk to the fairground to look for their friend, David. There are stalls and marquees filled with food and amusement arcades, and there are plenty of rides. The two friends head straight for the food stalls.

"Like, we need to keep up our strength," Shaggy explains as he fills his arms – and mouth – with food.

"Ri feel stronger ralready," Scooby agrees.

The friends stroll through the fair. Their search for David is very casual. There is so much to distract them!

"Hey! Blueberry pies! I haven't had one of those in a long time!" Shaggy says and heads towards the pie stand.

"Rou had one resterday," Scooby reminds him.

"Sure, but it was a whole twenty-four hours ago. That's a long time!" Shaggy replies.

Full of baked treats, Shaggy and Scooby wander towards the rides. A roller coaster rises high above the fairground.

"Hey, Scoob, maybe we can spot David from up there," Shaggy suggests and points to the top of the roller coaster.

"Rat's scary," Scooby whimpers.

"It's the highest point around here," Shaggy says. "Besides, it'll be fun."

"R-rokay, if rou say so," Scooby stammers.

Scooby follows Shaggy with knocking knees and chattering teeth. As they pass a small circus tent, a finger pokes out from the flaps. It makes a beckoning gesture at Scooby-Doo.

"*Pssst!*" a voice hisses.

"Rhoo, me?" Scooby-Doo asks. He looks around to see if the voice is speaking to someone else.

"Yes, you," the voice replies. "Come here..."

If Scooby talks to the hand, turn to page 18.
If Scooby sticks with Shaggy, turn to page 25.

The gang splits up and goes in different directions. Daphne and Velma walk up to the farmhouse. The front porch is rickety and creaks when they step on it.

"Jeepers, this doesn't sound safe," Daphne observes.

"If it's this run down on the outside, I wonder how bad it is on the inside," Velma wonders. She grabs the door handle and turns the rusty metal knob.

The door swings open on old, noisy hinges. **CREEEEAK!** The only thing that Daphne and Velma can see inside is darkness. Velma starts to take a step over the threshold. Suddenly Daphne stops her!

"Wait!" Daphne warns. She reaches into her handbag and pulls out a torch. "We're going to need this."

Daphne directs the bright beam around the gloomy room. All the furniture is covered with white sheets. The pale shapes look like huddled ghosts.

"Hello? David, are you here?" Daphne calls out. Silence is the only answer she gets.

"I don't think anyone has been here for a long time," Velma says. "Why were we invited to an abandoned farmhouse? There's a mystery here."

THUMP! The sound of something heavy rattles the floor under their feet.

"Jeepers! That sounded like it came from upstairs," Daphne gulps.

"No, I think it came from the basement," Velma says. "We better investigate both."

"You mean, split up?" Daphne asks. "But I always thought there was safety in numbers."

Daphne gives Velma an extra torch from her bag, and the two friends split up.

To follow Daphne upstairs, turn to page 21.

To Velma to the basement, turn to page 27.

The gang splits up to investigate the mystery of their missing friend. Fred decides to look in the barn. He walks towards the building and eyes it suspiciously. It doesn't look anything like the David Bush paintings that made it famous. The red paint is peeling, and the shutters are crooked on their hinges. Tiles are missing from the roof, and the silo leans like the Tower of Pisa.

"Scooby's right. This place looks haunted," Fred says. "Maybe this is a job for Mystery Inc. after all."

Fred pulls open one of the big barn doors to go inside. It doesn't budge. Then he notices the padlock on the latch. The metal is rusted.

"I guess I'll have to find another way in," Fred decides.

Fred walks around the barn until he discovers a loose shutter. He pulls it off the barn window. Fred peers through the grimy glass but can't see much of anything. He rubs the surface with his hand. Suddenly Fred sees a shape move inside the barn.

"David! Is that you?" Fred shouts. The figure does not answer.

Fred is surprised to discover that the window isn't locked. He opens it and crawls through the opening.

"It's as quiet as a grave in here," Fred says with a shudder. "And as dark as one, too. I wish I had a torch."

Suddenly a lamp flares to life in front of Fred's eyes. It illuminates a fearsome face!

"*Yaaa!*" Fred shouts in alarm. "A monster!"

If Fred runs up into the hayloft, turn to page 23.
If Fred jumps out of the window, turn to page 29.

"You can talk to the hand," the voice whispers.

"What's going on, buddy?" Shaggy asks as he walks back to Scooby-Doo. "Did you find a clue?"

Suddenly the hand withdraws behind the tent flap.

"Rit's the rand," Scooby replies. He points to the circus tent. There is a giant palm painted on the canvas.

"Cool! Like, it's a fortune-teller!" Shaggy says. "Let's check it out. Maybe she can tell us where David is."

Shaggy opens the tent flap and goes inside before Scooby-Doo can blink twice.

Scooby feels more nervous about being left outside the tent than he does about being inside the tent. He spins all four legs and races through the flaps to follow Shaggy.

It's very dark inside the tent. Scooby can't see anything. Suddenly he bumps into something!

"Yaaa!" something yells.

"Yaaa!" Scooby shrieks.

SSSIIIZZZTT! A match is struck, and its flame lights a candle. Shaggy and Scooby see an old woman sitting at a round table in the middle of the tent. A clear crystal ball reflects the candle's weak glow.

"I have something to tell you," the old woman says. She leans forwards and the candle flame makes her wrinkled face look like a Halloween mask. "You have a choice. Go back to the farm and find your friend, or stay here and meet your doom!"

If Shaggy and Scooby decide to head back to the farm, turn to page 32.

If Shaggy and Scooby decide to stay at the fair, turn to page 48.

Daphne heads up the stairs. The first floor of the farmhouse is just as deserted as the ground floor. Still, something has made a very large noise. Daphne hopes it's not a very large something!

"David, was that you?" Daphne asks loudly.

WHUMP! THUMP! The ceiling above Daphne's head sheds plaster dust. The broken light fixture shakes.

"Okay, there's definitely something in the attic," Daphne decides. "It's time to end this game of hide-and-seek."

Daphne's hand tightens around the torch as she starts to climb the narrow stairs up to the attic.

Daphne has one foot on the bottom step when she feels a hand clamp down on her shoulder. She jumps in alarm.

"Jeepers!" Daphne shouts. "Velma, I thought that you were going to investigate ... the ... basement ...?"

Turn the page.

Daphne's voice sticks in her throat as she turns around, expecting to see Velma. Instead she sees a looming grey shape with withered skin and glowing red eyes. It looks like a corpse. It reaches for her.

"*Yaaa!* A zombie!" Daphne yells.

She tries to run but her legs pinwheel in the air. The monster holds her by the collar and lifts her off the ground. Daphne twists around in a desperate attempt to escape. The ghoul's hand comes off! Daphne drops to the ground and runs!

If Daphne runs downstairs, turn to page 34.

If Daphne runs up to the attic, turn to page 52.

Fred is so startled by the frightening face that he doesn't think; he runs! His feet move so fast that they spin in place and kick up the loose straw. Fred leaves a cloud of dust behind him as he races through the barn.

BONK! Fred bounces off a stall door. **BAM!** He knocks into a stack of old crates. **BING! BANG!** Fred rebounds off everything in the barn like a pinball in a game.

Suddenly Fred sees a ladder. He climbs it up to the hayloft and dives behind a stack of stale hay bales. Fred shivers in fright, but he peeks over the bales. He wants to see what sort of monster Mystery Inc. has to face this time!

Fred peers down from the hayloft and looks around the barn. He is surprised to see that it's empty.

"Where did that monster go?" Fred wonders. "Did I imagine it?"

TAP! TAP! Something pokes Fred on the shoulder. He turns and sees the same ghoulish face.

Turn the page.

"Nope! I didn't imagine it!" Fred gulps.

"Why are you in here?" a rough voice demands.

A bright lamp is pushed close to Fred's face. He can barely see past the intense light, but he recognizes the caretaker.

"I'm searching for David Bush," Fred replies.

"He's not here. Leave!" the old man grumbles, then turns and is gone like a ghost.

"Where'd he go? How did he do that?" Fred gasps. "There's a mystery here, and I'm going to solve it!"

If Fred sees a mysterious light, turn to page 36.

If Fred follows a trail of footprints, turn to page 55.

Scooby-Doo stares at the creepy hand poking out of the tent flap. It looks weird. **SNIFF! SNIFF!** It smells weird.

"No ray!" Scooby decides. He runs and catches up with Shaggy.

"I've got tickets for the roller coaster," Shaggy says. "We can see the entire fairground from up there. Maybe we'll spot David."

The friends climb aboard the ride and the cars start the clattering journey to the first summit. Shaggy and Scooby are so busy looking around for David that they don't pay attention to the passengers in the cars behind them.

TAP! TAP! Something pokes Shaggy and Scooby on their shoulders. The friends turn around and see something more terrifying than the first plunge down the roller coaster tracks!

"*Yaaaa!*" they yell, and it's not because of the ride.

Turn the page.

"Zombies!" Shaggy shrieks.

The creatures make a grab at Scooby and Shaggy as the roller coaster banks into a sharp turn. The zombies miss! Their skeletal arms grasp thin air. The friends try to escape the ride, but the lap bars are locked tight.

The roller coaster screeches through a double loop and streaks down a second hill. The cars speed through a tunnel with flashing lights. The friends come out with their eyes spinning and seeing stars. So do the zombies.

At last the roller coaster splashes into an artificial lake. Water sprays up and soaks the riders. Shaggy and Scooby shake off the water. The zombies just moan in misery.

"That was refreshing!" Shaggy exclaims. "Now let's get out of here, Scoobs!"

"Which ray?" Scooby asks.

If Shaggy and Scooby run into the art exhibition marquee, turn to page 68.

If Shaggy and Scooby run into the House of Mirrors, turn to page 86.

While Daphne investigates upstairs, Velma decides to explore downstairs. She holds the extra torch in her hand and tries to stop it shaking. The house is very spooky. It's not like David's famous paintings at all!

Velma creeps cautiously through the living room to the kitchen. The curtains are closed on all the windows and the room is very dark. Suddenly Velma feels something brush her neck! The curtains move as if stroked by an invisible hand. She jumps in surprise.

"Jinkies!" Velma shouts. Then she notices that the basement door is open. "Oh, it's just a draft from the basement."

Velma goes to the door and peers down the dark stairs.

"Hello? Is anyone down there?" Velma calls down the stairs. She hears no human reply.

Turn the page.

CLANK! Suddenly there is the sound of metal hitting metal. Velma follows the noise down into the basement. Velma thinks she hears whispering. She swings the torch beam around the room. The light illuminates stacks of cardboard boxes and lots of spider webs. Everything is covered with dust – except for an old wardrobe.

"Why is that piece of furniture so clean?" Velma wonders. "There's a mystery here."

Curious, Velma reaches for the handle. Before she can open the door of the wardrobe, it swings open all by itself! A ghoulish face stares out at her.

If Velma runs upstairs, turn to page 71.

If Velma gets trapped in the basement, turn to page 89.

A scowling face glares at Fred. The lamp's harsh light casts sharp shadows on the frowning forehead and snarling mouth.

Fred is so surprised that he jumps back out of the barn window. Something grabs his shirt and tries to stop him escaping, but Fred tears free and runs as fast as his spinning legs can carry him.

"B-bushytail Farm is h-haunted," Fred stammers as he hides behind an old tractor. "I've got to tell the rest of the gang."

Fred turns around to head for the farmhouse but stops in his tracks. A group of ghouls stands in his path! They are as thin as skeletons. Their skin is as grey and wrinkled as an old elephant, and their hair hangs in patches from scabby scalps. The creatures reach for Fred with grasping fingers.

"*Yaaaa!* Zombies!" Fred yells.

Fred runs away from the zombies! Unfortunately he runs in the opposite direction of the farmhouse.

Turn the page.

The menacing monsters shuffle after Fred. Their legs are stiff and their limbs are creaky. They do not move very quickly. As Fred flees across the farmyard he takes a chance and glances behind him. He sees the stumbling zombies struggling to chase him at the speed of a tortoise. Suddenly Fred does not feel so afraid.

"It looks like I have already outrun those zombies," Fred concludes. "I can circle around them and find Daphne and Velma in the farmhouse."

Fred is ready to sprint to his goal when he hears a roaring sound. He freezes as he sees a startling sight.

"As Scooby-Doo would say – ruh-roh!" Fred gulps.

If a haunted Mystery Machine chases Fred, turn to page 73.
If zombies drive the tractor and chase Fred, turn to page 92.

Shaggy and Scooby-Doo leave the fortune-teller's tent.

"Rikes!" Scooby says with a shiver.

"Like, I need a snack to calm my nerves," Shaggy declares.

"**SNIFF, SNIFF!** Rwaffles," Scooby announces and poses like a hunting dog pointing to its target.

"**SNIFF, SNIFF!** And I smell blueberry syrup," Shaggy says as he strikes the same stance. "Two noses are better than one, eh, Scoobs?"

The two friends race to the source of the delicious aroma. They load up on stacks of waffles with all the trimmings. They can barely see where they're going as they balance the towers of food.

"Like, this should last us until we get back to the farm," Shaggy says.

CHOMP! CHOMP! GULP! The friends gobble up the waffles like two vacuum cleaners.

"Oops, I might have miscalculated," Shaggy shrugs. He is still hungry.

"Hee hee. Re, too," Scooby giggles as he slurps the syrup from his snout.

"I think we need a refill," Shaggy decides. "Like, we can head back to Bushytail Farm later."

"Rokay," Shaggy agrees as his tongue wags hungrily.

"You must leave now!" the old fortune-teller screeches as she suddenly blocks their path.

"Zoinks!" Shaggy yelps in surprise and leaps into Scooby's arms.

"Go away!" the woman warns.

"Funny, that creepy caretaker at the farm said the same thing," Shaggy says as the fortune-teller walks away. "Scoobs, I think I smell a mystery!"

"Ruh-roh" Scooby whimpers.

Turn to page 38.

Daphne wriggles loose from the grisly ghoul and runs down the staircase. The passageway is very narrow, and she bumps her shoulders against the walls. The torch jarrs and almost falls out of her hands.

Daphne reaches the bottom of the attic stairs and risks taking a glance back at the zombie. It lumbers down the steps in plodding pursuit. Its stiff legs force the creature to go down the stairs one by one.

"It's time I took the express," Daphne decides. She leaps up onto the stair banister leading down to the living room.

Daphne slides down the banister like a surfer riding a wave. She speeds along the banister faster and faster. Suddenly she sees the post at the bottom.

"Uh-oh! End of the line," Daphne gasps.

Daphne reaches the end of the banister and dives off the end. She sails over the post like a bird in flight.

Using her gymnastic skills, Daphne tucks her body into a ball and somersaults in the air. Then she thrusts out her legs for landing.

SPROING! Daphne hits the sofa cushions and bounces back into the air! The sheet covering the sofa flies up, too. Daphne spreads out her arms and performs a perfect swan dive. Then she twists her body in mid-air and lands on her feet.

"I knew I could do that landing!" Daphne says.

The sheet gently flutters down and lands on top of her just as the zombie thumps into the room. It looks around for its prey, but Daphne is hidden under the sheet.

Turn to page 42.

"It's the second time that guy has told Mystery Inc. to leave Bushytail Farm. And that's exactly why I think we should stay," Fred decides.

Fred starts to climb down the ladder but stops when he sees a sliver of light. It is shining between the old, cracked barn wall.

"I wonder where that's coming from," Fred mutters. "There's nothing on the other side of that wall except..."

Suddenly a trio of ghouls lunge out of a hidden door in the barn wall.

"...zombies?!" Fred gasps.

Fred jumps backwards to avoid their ghastly grip. He forgets he's on the ladder and falls!

Fred grabs a rung of the ladder to stop his fall. The zombies snatch at him from the hayloft.

"Wh-where did they come from?" Fred stammers.

The creepy creatures grab Fred's wrist and start to pull him towards them.

"No way, zombay!" Fred rhymes as he twists out of their gruesome grasp. He grabs a nearby rope and swings like a monkey. "Just call me Tarzan of the *oooofff*!"

Fred's triumphant cheer is cut short as he slams into a beam. He slides down to the ground and crumples into a limp heap. The zombies scurry down from the hayloft and stand over Fred like waiting vultures.

Turn to page 45.

"Follow that fortune-teller!" Shaggy says.

Scooby and Shaggy sneak after the old woman. She goes into a large marquee and the friends peek inside. They immediately regret it. Gnarly hands grab them! A crowd of creepy creatures surrounds the two friends.

"Zoinks! Zombies!" Shaggy gulps as the grinning ghouls close in.

"Run!" Scooby shrieks.

Shaggy and Scooby put their legs in reverse and speed backwards out of the marquee. The zombies rush out in hot pursuit.

As soon as the people at the fair see the ghouls, everyone screams and starts to run. Stalls are trampled. Food flies. Shaggy and Scooby catch the soaring snacks and shovel them into their mouths.

"Rummy!" Scooby burps.

"That gives me an idea," Shaggy says. He eyes a stack of pies in his hand.

"Hey, Scoobs! Let's play a game!" Shaggy shouts. "Knock over a zombie and win a prize."

Shaggy throws a pie at one of the ghouls. It hits the creature in the face and the monster falls to the ground. Shaggy pumps his fist in triumph. Seeing Shaggy's success, Scooby uses all four paws to toss fair food at the marauding monsters. *SMACK! SMACK! SMACK!* Zombies fall like bowling pins.

"Rahoo! Rike!" Scooby cheers. Suddenly he sees a swarm of ghastly ghouls heading in his direction. "Ruh-roh!"

"Look out *beloooow*!" Shaggy warns as he swings down a zip wire and bombards the zombies with food and stuffed animals. Scooby scampers away as the creatures are buried.

Turn the page.

"You meddling kids! I told you to leave! Now you've ruined my perfect plan," the fortune-teller shouts as she stands next to the mound of motionless zombies.

"*SNIFF, SNIFF!* Hey! Rake!" Scooby-Doo says as he pokes his scent-sensitive nose into the pile. He chomps down and comes up with a mask in his mouth.

"The fake zombies were supposed to scare people away from the fair and the farm," the fortune-teller confesses. "My brother is the farm's caretaker. We wanted the land on both properties so we could build a housing development."

"Shaggy! Scooby! We found David back at the farm!" Fred shouts as he and the rest of the Mystery Inc. gang arrive. "But you solved the mystery!"

"And your reward is all the hotdogs you can eat!" David declares.

THE END

To follow another path, turn to page 11.

Daphne stands perfectly still as the zombie shuffles around the room. She can see it through the thin fabric. Daphne is surprised when she watches the ghoul take out a mobile phone and speak into it!

"Since when does a zombie use a mobile phone?" Daphne wonders. Then she answers her own question. "When it's a fake!"

Suddenly Daphne is not so afraid of the big bad ghoul. She decides it is time to play a trick on the counterfeit creature.

"**WOOOO!**" Daphne moans and shakes the sheet covering her. It makes a sound like a bat flapping its wings.

The zombie stops in its tracks.

"W–what was that?" it stammers in fright.

"**WOOOO!**" Daphne moans again. "You trespass in my domain!"

The zombie turns around and sees the pale shape of the shivering sheet in the dark room.

Daphne turns on the torch and illuminates the cloth from underneath. She waves her arms and makes the fabric flap.

"*Yaaa!* This place is haunted!" the zombie screams. Its legs spin like a windmill as it tries to escape.

"Not so fast," Daphne declares as she trips the ghoul with her handbag.

The creature crashes to the ground and a mask flies off its head!

"Just as I thought. You're not a zombie, you're a fake!" Daphne says.

"What's all the commotion?" Velma says as she runs up the stairs from the basement. "I've found David downstairs."

Turn the page.

"What's going on here?" Fred asks as he runs into the house from the barn.

"That's what I'm about to find out," Daphne says. She ties up the fake zombie with the sheet.

"You meddling kids!" the man grumbles. "I wanted to turn Bushytail Farm into a tourist attraction, but David wouldn't let me."

"Cousin James!" David gasps.

"So, in revenge, you scared people away with your zombie disguise to ruin the farm's reputation," Daphne concludes.

"And I would have gotten away with it, too," the man mutters.

"Another case solved by Mystery Inc.!" Fred declares.

THE END

To follow another path, turn to page 11.

"*Ooooh,* what hit me?" Fred wonders as he slowly wakes up. He looks around and sees that he is tied to a chair inside a laboratory.

"Welcome back to the land of the living," the old caretaker says. The trio of zombies stands behind him.

"Wow! I can't believe you hid all this on Bushytail Farm!" Fred exclaims.

"What? How do you know that?" the caretaker says.

"You couldn't have taken me too far from the barn," Fred replies. "We're either under the farmhouse or..."

"We're in the silo!" the man snaps. "And you should have left when I told you to!"

"Not a chance! Where there's a mystery, there's Mystery Inc.!" Fred proclaims.

Turn the page.

"Mystery Inc. is nothing but a bunch of troublesome teenagers," the caretaker says. "I didn't think much about it when my cousin David invited you here."

"Okay, now I get it. You're an angry relative looking for revenge … or maybe a gold mine or an inheritance. I lose track sometimes," Fred says as he secretly tries to untie the ropes that bind him to the chair.

"None of the above," the old man declares. He reaches up to his scalp, grabs a fistful of hair, and yanks off a mask. The zombies behind him do the same.

"*Awww!* Why did you do that?" Fred complains. "I could have figured it out for myself. I hate spoilers!"

Fred leaps into action! He breaks free and tackles the fake caretaker. The false zombies are knocked down, too. As quick as he can, Fred ties up the imposters with the rope.

"You meddling kid! My experiment is ruined," the unmasked man groans. "I built this secret lab to create a special popcorn from Bushytail Farm corn. The patent is worth millions!"

"Why not work with your cousin David?" Fred asks.

"He's an artist, not a scientist," the man grumbles.

"So you found some laboratory assistants to help you," Fred concludes. He looks at the other three prisoners. "I bet dressing up as zombies wasn't in the job description."

The men shake their heads.

"Another mystery is solved!" Fred cheers. "Now, is there a sample of that popcorn? I'm sure Scooby-Doo will love it!"

THE END

To follow another path, turn to page 11.

Suddenly the candle goes out and the fortune-teller's tent becomes as dark as night.

"Well, here we are, left in the dark. Again." Shaggy sighs.

"Ret's ro," Scooby whimpers.

The two friends grope around and finally find their way out of the tent. Outside, things are not much brighter. Gloomy storm clouds gather over the fairground.

"It's as dark out here as it was in there," Shaggy observes.

"Ruh-roh, it rooks like rain," Scooby warns.

CRAAAACK·A·BOOOOM! A loud clap of thunder explodes on top of them. The shock wave nearly knocks the friends off their feet. Sheets of rain start to fall.

"Like, we've got to get out of this storm!" Shaggy says.

Shaggy and Scooby turn around to run back into the fortune-teller's tent, but it isn't there anymore!

The fortune-teller's tent has disappeared mysteriously, so Shaggy and Scooby run inside the nearby showground pavilion. They are shocked at what they see. All of the animals are as grey as old ashes. Their eyes are vacant and staring. The cows don't moo, they moan.

"These cows look like, like..." Shaggy starts to say.

"Zombies!" Scooby finishes for him and points his paw.

A crowd of creepy creatures staggers towards Shaggy and Scooby and surround the two friends. Shaggy and Scooby-Doo hug each other and tremble in fright.

"We're doomed! The fortune-teller was right!" Shaggy wails.

"I knew you boys wouldn't listen to me," a voice says. Shaggy and Scooby blink in surprise when they see the fortune-teller standing behind the ghouls. "I hate being right."

Turn the page.

The old woman tosses her crystal ball at the zombies. It shoots out thick black smoke. Shaggy and Scooby are engulfed in the cloud. So are the zombies.

"Run!" the fortune-teller shouts at the friends.

Shaggy and Scooby race towards the glowing red exit sign in the dense smoke. They burst through the doors and out into the rain. The fortune-teller is waiting for them.

"It's not over yet," she warns them as zombies pour out of the pavilion.

"Like, who are you?" Shaggy asks.

"You're Mystery Inc. – work it out," the old lady grins. "But first, we've got to get away from these gruesome ghouls."

Turn to page 58.

Daphne escapes the zombie by running up another set of stairs to the attic. She hopes there is a door with a lock! The staircase is narrow and steep. Daphne bumps her shoulders against the walls with almost every step. The torch is jostled and nearly falls out of her hand. Finally Daphne reaches the top of the stairs.

"Thank goodness the attic has a door! I can hide in there!" Daphne sighs with relief.

Daphne turns the old door handle, but the door won't open. She jiggles and twists it.

"Oh, no! It's locked! And I don't have the key!" Daphne moans.

A gurgling moan rises up from the bottom of the stairs. Daphne hears the sound of heavy feet on the stair treads. *THUMP! THUMP! THUMP!* The zombie lumbers closer and closer.

The creature staggers slowly up the stairs towards Daphne. The locked door stands between her and safety.

"There's got to be something in my handbag that I can use to open this door," Daphne mumbles to herself as she stirs her hand around inside the bag.

"This might work," Daphne decides and holds up a ballpoint pen in the torch beam.

Trying to ignore the thumping sound of zombie footsteps coming up the stairs, Daphne pokes the pen into the door lock. Daphne wiggles the pen around until she hears a click. She grabs the handle and opens the door just in time!

Turn the page.

Daphne runs through the door and into the attic. She slams the door behind her and leans her body against it. The zombie pounds on the door with his fists.

"That was close!" Daphne gasps as she bolts the door behind her. "But I'm not out of trouble yet."

Daphne swings the torch beam around the attic. The room is dark and full of strange shapes. She hopes the shapes are just draped sheets like downstairs. Suddenly the beam illuminates more zombies!

"*Yaaa!*" Daphne shouts and jumps in surprise.

But the creatures do not move. They hang like limp socks on the wall of the attic. Daphne pokes one with her ballpoint pen. It collapses to the floor and lies still.

Turn to page 62.

Fred climbs down from the hayloft. The old caretaker scared him at first, but now Fred is curious.

"That man is trying very hard to get me to leave. That's why I'm going to stay," Fred decides.

Fred looks around the barn for clues. He spots some footprints going into a stall. Fred follows the trail until it ends against the back wall of the enclosure.

"That's weird. The footprints vanish into thin air, just like the old man," Fred observes. "There must be a secret passage!"

Fred runs his hands over the old barn wall, looking for a hidden latch. All he gets is splinters. Suddenly Fred trips on something in the straw. He falls face-first and makes a surprising discovery!

Fred sprawls in the straw, but he has solved the mystery of the vanishing footprints.

"There's a latch to a trapdoor," Fred gasps. "The secret door is in the floor!"

Turn the page.

He gets to his feet and grabs the latch handle. Fred pulls open the hatch. He can just make out the shape of a ladder leading down into the gloom. Fred leans over for a closer look. Suddenly a pair of eyeballs blinks back at him!

"*Yaaa!*" Fred shouts in alarm. He tries to back away from the trapdoor but slips on the loose straw. It's like ice under his feet and he slips and falls right into the hole!

THUMP! Fred crashes into a large body in the dark. Even though Fred can't see anything, he knows that whatever it is, it isn't human! His face is covered with its slobbery drool.

"Fred! Are we glad to see you!" Shaggy cries and hugs his friend.

"Reah! Re too!" Scooby-Doo whimpers and wraps his paws around Shaggy and Fred.

"Shaggy? Scooby? What are you guys doing down here?" Fred asks, surprised. What he thought was a monster in the dark turns out to be his two friends.

"Like, we sort of got lost on the way to the fairground," Shaggy admits. "There are all sorts of creepy tunnels down here."

"You found a clue to the mystery of the missing caretaker," Fred says.

"We did? How about that, Scoobs?" Shaggy laughs. "We did something right!"

Turn to page 65.

Shaggy, Scooby and the fortune-teller take off towards the nearest amusement arcade. Inside, they hide among the stuffed toy prizes. Shaggy disguises himself as a giant panda bear. Scooby puts a pair of fuzzy rabbit ears on his head and pretends to be a bunny. The fortune-teller grabs a toy unicorn and holds it up in front of her face.

"This isn't camouflage, this is crazy!" the old lady complains.

"Hee-hee!" Scooby chuckles.

"Zoinks! The zombies are coming!" Shaggy yells.

The ghouls spread out to look for their prey. Some of them hobble up to the amusement arcade. They pick up some balls from a game and start throwing them at the targets. The zombies have a terrible aim. The balls hit the stuffed toys instead of the targets!

"*OW! OW!*" Shaggy yelps as the balls knock off his panda disguise.

"Ruh-roh!" Scooby gulps.

The zombies swarm all over Shaggy and Scooby-Doo like ants on a sticky bun. The friends try to run but are weighed down by the gruesome ghouls. There is no escape!

"You meddling kids!" a voice declares with a strange accent. "You have interrupted my experiment."

Shaggy and Scooby poke their heads out from the pile of zombies. They see a figure wearing a dark cloak and a black hat. The brim of the hat hides the person's face in shadow.

"Like, we're sorry. We were just looking for our friend," Shaggy explains.

"Well, you found trouble!" the figure snaps. He holds a spray can in front of their noses. "This special gas will make you into mindless drones, and you will obey my every command!"

"Oh, I get it! These aren't zombies, they're test subjects," Shaggy realizes.

"Correct! And you will become one of them!" the figure says.

Turn the page.

"Not so fast, Dr X!" the fortune-teller commands as she leaps out from under the toys.

The old woman throws a small crystal ball at the spray can and knocks it to the ground. The container shoots a jet of gas into the figure's hidden face! The mysterious stranger turns zombie-grey and collapses to the ground.

"Thanks for helping me capture the rogue scientist, Dr X," the fortune-teller says as she removes her old-lady mask to reveal a young face. "I'm Agent Michelle Barr."

"Scoobs and I are glad to help. Like, what did we do?" Shaggy replies.

"You made Dr X come out of hiding so I could catch him in the act," Agent Barr explains. "You guys are very talented."

Shaggy and Scooby give a high five. "Scooby-Dooby-Doo!" they shout.

THE END

To follow another path, turn to page 11.

Daphne jumps backwards in surprise as the boneless ghoul drops to the floor of the attic like a sack of grain. ***WHOMP!***

"That isn't a zombie," Daphne realizes. "It's a clue to this mystery."

Suddenly the attic door bursts open with a crashing ***BLAM!*** There isn't just one zombie anymore. The creature that chased Daphne up the stairs has brought along some fearsome friends! The gruesome ghouls stretch out their arms towards Daphne.

"*Yaaa!*" Daphne shrieks and tries to run.

She doesn't get far. Daphne accidentally runs into an old art easel. Then she stumbles and bounces off a stack of stored paintings. The canvases scatter on the floor. Beautiful landscape paintings spread out all over the attic.

"*Ahhh!*" one of the zombies moans and kneels next to the paintings.

"*Miiiiine!*" another zombie hisses like a snake as it pushes the other zombie away.

"*Nooooo!*" a third zombie shrieks.

Daphne hides behind a dresser in a dark corner of the attic and watches the zombies as they fight over the paintings.

"That is not normal," Daphne realizes. "Since when are zombies art collectors?"

Concealed in the shadows, Daphne watches the gaunt ghouls battle each other for possession of the paintings.

"That's because they aren't zombies, they're fakes! They want David's paintings!" Daphne gasps.

Then she frowns with determination. "I don't think so!"

Daphne is determined to save her friend's paintings. She creeps over to the zombie that fell off the wall.

"This isn't a zombie, it's a costume!" Daphne discovers. "Two can play this game!"

Daphne puts the zombie mask over her head and zips up the creepy outfit.

Turn the page.

Daphne jumps out at the gang of thieves.

"*Wooooo!* I'm the ghost of Bushytail Farm!" Daphne shouts.

All the zombies pull off their masks and run! Only one of them stays. He can't let go of the paintings. The Mystery Inc. gang arrives just as Daphne pulls off the man's fake zombie face.

"Jeff Kelly! You wrote the art book about Bushytail Farm!" Velma says.

"I used fake zombies to scare everyone away so I could look for David's lost paintings," Jeff confesses. "The art could have been mine if it wasn't for you meddling kids!"

THE END

To follow another path, turn to page 11.

"I'm sure if we find the caretaker, we'll find our friend, David," Fred decides.

"Like, why don't we just ask those guys," Shaggy suggests and points to a trio of shadowy figures. But as soon as they step out of the gloom, Shaggy sees they aren't "guys" at all. "Uh-oh, they're zombies!"

"Run!" Fred yells.

The friends clamber over each other to climb up the ladder. **BOOM!** The trapdoor slams shut above their heads.

"Ruh-roh," Scooby gulps.

"We're doomed," Shaggy moans.

"Don't worry. We can outrun them. Zombies are slow," Fred says.

The creepy creatures rush towards the friends and grab them in a ghoulish grip.

"Well, zombies are slow in films," Fred groans.

"Like, now what?" Shaggy asks. "We need a plan!"

Turn the page.

"Sorry, guys, I'm out of plans," Fred sighs. "We're doomed."

The zombies march Fred, Shaggy and Scooby through the dark tunnels.

"Wow, it's a maze down here," Fred observes. "No wonder you two got lost."

The friends are taken to an underground room filled with office furniture and computer equipment. Sitting behind a desk is the old caretaker. He jumps to his feet when he sees the Mystery Inc. gang.

"You idiots!" the man shouts at the zombies. "Why did you bring those meddling kids here?"

"Because that was my plan," Fred announces. "I wanted to get to the bottom of this mystery. I had no idea it would be so far underground."

Fred twists around and snatches the masks off two of the zombies. Once they are exposed as human, they run away. The caretaker is left without reinforcements.

The old man sits down in his chair, defeated.

"Now that you've discovered my headquarters, my plan is ruined," the caretaker grumbles. "I was going to use these tunnels for my smuggling operation."

"You used those fake zombies to frighten away visitors," Fred deduces. "Plus, you let Bushytail Farm get run down so no one would want to visit."

"Yes. And I would have gotten away with it if it hadn't been for you meddling Mystery Inc. kids," the man complains.

"So, like, where's our friend, David?" Shaggy wants to know.

"I sent him on a European art tour," the caretaker says. "He's been gone for months."

"Then who sent us the invitation to visit the farm?" Fred wonders.

"It wasn't me," the old man shrugs.

"Rit's another mystery!" Scooby says.

THE END

To follow another path, turn to page 11.

Shaggy and Scooby make a hasty retreat away from the roller coaster. They run through the deserted fairground looking for the exit. Soon they lose all sense of direction.

"We've been going around in circles," Shaggy pants as the friends come to a halt.

"Re're lost!" Scooby moans.

Suddenly they see the ghouls lumbering towards them.

"Zoinks! It's the zombies! They found us!" Shaggy shrieks.

"Re're doomed!" Scooby whimpers.

The friends run into the nearest marquee, hoping to hide. They are surprised by what they find.

"David!" Shaggy shouts.

Their friend stands in front of a large landscape painting. He has brushes in his hand and stands next to a table filled with tubes of oil paint.

"Oh hi, guys! I'm just trying to fix this painting. I can't seem to get the lighting right," David says.

Shaggy and Scooby realize that they are in an art exhibition marquee. David's paintings fill the space.

"No wonder we couldn't see David from up on the roller coaster! He was inside this marquee the whole time," Shaggy gasps as he smacks his forehead with the palm of his hand.

"Where's the rest of the gang?" David asks.

Suddenly the pack of zombies bursts into the marquee. They surround Shaggy, Scooby and David.

"That's not the gang," David gulps.

The creatures lunge at the friends. David grabs the big painting he is working on and smashes it down over the heads of the creatures.

Turn to page 75.

The frightful sight of a zombie in the wardrobe startles Velma, and she drops the torch. She can hear it hit the ground, but she can't see it. Everything around her is pitch black.

"Jinkies! This is as bad as losing my glasses!" Velma moans as she gropes around the floor. Suddenly she feels something cold and clammy grab her ankle.

"*Yaaa!*" Velma yells and twists out of the zombie's ghoulish grip.

Desperately, Velma crawls towards a single spot of light – the basement door at the top of the stairs. As soon as her hands touch the wooden steps, Velma knows where she is. She climbs up the stairs on all fours.

SLAM! Velma shuts the basement door behind her and presses her weight against it.

Velma does not have time to catch her breath after her narrow escape. **WHAM! WHAM!** The basement door shudders behind her as the ghoul slams its fists against the wood.

Turn the page.

"Why is there a zombie in the basement?" Velma gasps. "And how did it get up the stairs so fast? Zombies are supposed to be slow."

Velma decides to think about those questions later! She grabs a kitchen chair and wedges it under the doorknob.

"The chair-under-the-door trick always works in films. I hope it works in real life," Velma says. "But, just in case it doesn't, I need a plan."

Turn to page 79.

"The Mystery Machine! It started up all by itself!" Fred gasps. "How? It doesn't have a remote ignition button."

The lime-green van spins its wheels in the dirt and revs its engine. It sounds like the growl of a wild animal. The headlights blaze into life. They look like the glaring eyes of a predatory beast. The Mystery Machine lunges towards Fred.

"It's alive!" Fred yells. He turns and runs right at the zombies.

The clumsy creatures do not get out of the way in time. Fred barrels into them. So does the Mystery Machine. The zombies are tossed high into the air. They flap their stiff arms like birds, but they are more like flightless penguins than soaring swans. They drop back down and land on top of the van.

The zombies cling to the Mystery Machine with boney fingers as the van chases Fred around the farmyard. He can barely keep in front of the mad machine.

Turn the page.

He jumps up onto a fence and runs along it to get out of the van's path, but the Mystery Machine slams into the side of the fence and makes Fred lose his balance. He falls into the pigpen and comes up covered in swine slime.

"*Eeeeww!*" Fred groans.

"Fred! What's going on?" Daphne shouts. She stands outside of the farmhouse with Velma and their friend, David. "We found David in the basement then heard all this noise!"

Suddenly the Mystery Machine pivots on its back wheels and races off towards the farmhouse.

"Jinkies!" Velma yells as she barely dodges the van.

"Jeepers!" Daphne gasps as she grabs David and jumps out of the way.

Turn to page 82.

"I didn't really like that painting anyway," David states as he, Shaggy and Scooby flee.

The trio run out of the back of the exhibition marquee and jump onto David's quad bike Shaggy grabs the wheel and puts the pedal to the floor. The quad pulls away at a plodding ten miles an hour.

"Like, this isn't much faster than those zombies," Shaggy observes.

David shrugs. "There's no need for speed at Bushytail Farm."

The friends drive back to the farm. They are met by the creepy caretaker, which makes David angry.

"What are you still doing here? I fired you for not taking care of Bushytail while I was travelling," David growls. "You let the place become a ruin."

"You should have stayed away. All of you," the man grumbles. "Now I have to take drastic measures."

Turn the page.

The old man speaks into a small microphone.

A moment later zombies pour out of the house and the barn. Shaggy and Scooby are shocked to see that Fred, Daphne and Velma are part of the gruesome group. They have been turned into grey-faced ghouls, too!

"Now it's your turn to follow my commands," the caretaker says as he dangles a hypnotic pendulum in front of Shaggy, Scooby and David. Their eyes swirl in their sockets. Scooby-Doo blinks in confusion.

"Yes, master," Shaggy and David moan. "Your wish is our command."

"Follow me. I have a fortune to claim," the caretaker proclaims. He gestures and all the zombies shamble after him. Scooby-Doo stays.

"What?" the old man shouts. "My hypnotic power doesn't work on animals. That canny canine fooled me!"

Scooby-Doo jumps over the zombies and lands on top of the creepy caretaker.

The pendulum is knocked out of the caretaker's hands. Suddenly all the ghouls' faces turn back to healthy human faces. Shaggy, Fred, Daphne and Velma get up and hug their friend.

"Scooby-Doo, you saved us!" Daphne says as she kisses the pooch on the snout.

"It's a good thing you're a hound and not a human," Velma laughs and hugs Scooby.

"You meddling kids! I turned people into zombies to be my workers in the gem mine that's under the farm and the fairground," the man confesses.

"There's wealth under Bushytail Farm?" David exclaims. "Now I can afford to turn the farmhouse into a boutique hotel. Thanks, Mystery Incorporated!"

THE END

To follow another path, turn to page 11.

Velma looks around the deserted farmhouse kitchen for a way to defend herself against the zombie.

"Where's a frying pan or a rolling pin when I need one?" Velma wonders aloud as she searches through the cupboards and drawers. "Maybe it's time for Plan B!"

BWAM! BWAM! The basement door shudders on its hinges as the creature tries to break it down. *SMASH!* Suddenly the wood splinters. The door bursts wide open. Instead of one zombie, now there are four gruesome ghouls!

"Get her!" they shout.

Velma is surrounded. The mouldy monsters reach out to grab her.

"Jinkies! I'd better think of a Plan B – fast!" Velma gulps.

Velma backs into the pantry of the farmhouse kitchen. The shelves are full of tins of food.

Turn to page 80.

"I think this stuff is older than you guys!" Velma chuckles as she tosses the tins of food at the zombies. ***THUMP! THWAK! BONK!***

"*Owww! Owww!*" the zombies howl as they fall onto the kitchen floor.

"You're not zombies, you're fakes!" Velma proclaims. "I realized it when you chased me up the stairs. Real zombies don't run that fast."

"R-real zombies? Where?" the ghouls stammer as Velma stands over them. She puts her foot on the chest of one of them, leans over, and pulls off his mask. A human face is revealed.

"Who are you and what are you doing?" Velma demands. "Wait. Let me solve the mystery."

"The solution to this mystery is simple," she says "You're all David's relatives and want something on Bushytail Farm."

"Close enough," the unmasked man reveals. "We're his cousins, and we teamed up to find the buried treasure!"

"What buried treasure?" asks David Bush as he comes into the kitchen with the rest of the Mystery Inc. gang.

"There's a fortune in gold from a secret mine on the property. It's a family legend," one of the fake zombies says.

"That legend isn't real. I made it up for the Bushytail books!" David declares.

"Another myth busted, and another mystery solved," Velma concludes.

THE END

To follow another path, turn to page II.

The van misses Daphne, Velma and David and screeches to a halt. It revs its engine as if trying to decide who to chase next. The zombies slide off the roof of the van and collapse on the ground. They try to get to their feet, but they are too dizzy from the wild ride.

"*Yaaa!* Zombies!" Daphne shrieks. "Scooby was right! Bushytail Farm is haunted!"

Suddenly the Mystery Machine roars to life and spins its wheels. It gets a grip and takes off towards Fred! He slips and slides in the squishy mud but his feet just spin in one spot.

"I'm doomed!" Fred gulps.

"He's doomed!" his friends moan.

"Scooby-Dooby-Doo!" comes a triumphant yell.

"Yeah! Like, what he said!" echoes another voice.

Suddenly Scooby and Shaggy land on top of the Mystery Machine. They wrap a rope around the front bumper like reins on a racehorse.

The friends pull up on the rope. The van stops just in front of Fred! It pants out puffs of exhaust fumes and then settles down to a gentle idle.

"There, there, big fella," Shaggy says as he pats the van on the roof as if calming a spooked horse. Fred, Daphne, Velma and David join their friends next to the Mystery Machine.

"Wow! That was a really great roundup!" Daphne says.

"But why did the Mystery Machine act like that?" Fred asks.

"I can solve that mystery. Look!" Velma declares. She points to an antenna attached to the van.

"That antenna was receiving remote control signals," Velma announces. "Someone used the Mystery Machine to scare us."

"Like, those zombies are scaring me and Scoobs just fine!" Shaggy whimpers.

Turn to page 85.

"Reah! I rate zombies," Scooby-Doo agrees.

"Don't worry, those aren't zombies," Velma declares. She pulls the mask off one of the ghouls. A pair of remote control glasses falls from his face.

"Chase Carson!" Fred gasps. "You're a champion racing car driver."

"I invented a new remote control technology and wanted to build a factory for robot cars on this property, but that artist guy wouldn't sell it to me," Chase confesses and glares at David.

"So you hired fake zombies to scare people and devalue the farm," Daphne deduces.

"And I would have gotten away with it except for you meddling kids," Chase grumbles.

"Another mystery solved!" Shaggy says. He grabs the remote control to the Mystery Machine. "My turn to drive!"

VROOOOOMMMM!

THE END

To follow another path, turn to page 11.

Shaggy and Scooby jump out of the roller coaster car and sprint as fast as their legs can spin. The zombies struggle off the ride and stumble after the two friends. When the people at the fair see the ghastly ghouls they scream and run away! Suddenly Shaggy and Scooby are the only humans left at the fair. It's easy for the zombies to spot them.

"We can hide in here, pal!" Shaggy says as he grabs Scooby and pulls him into the House of Mirrors.

Distorted images of the teen and his dog stretch and shrink in the strange light inside the tent. The friends wave their hands and stick out their tongues at their silly reflections.

"Hey Scoobs, you're nine feet tall!" Shaggy laughs at his friend's extra-long shape.

"Hee-hee! Rou have two heads!" Scooby giggles.

Shaggy's eyes go wide in alarm as he looks in the fun-house mirror and sees that he has grown an extra head! It is grey and wrinkled and looks like a rotting raisin.

"*Yaaa!* I'm turning into a mutant zombie!" Shaggy yells. Suddenly a second pair of arms reaches around and clutches him. "*Yaaa!* Like, now I have four arms, too!"

"Rit's the zombies!" Scooby yelps and jumps into Shaggy's arms. Only one pair of limbs catches him.

"*Yaaa!*" the friends shout together as the creepy creatures surround them.

"Like, this fun house isn't fun anymore," Shaggy announces. "Let's get out of here!"

The pals burst through the circle of ghouls and run as fast as they can!

Shaggy and Scooby race out of the House of Mirrors. The fairground is deserted. All the visitors have fled in fright. Shaggy and Scooby do the same!

They run towards the exit. They have safety in their sights when the delicious aroma of pastries reaches their noses. Their feet halt in their tracks. *SCREEECH! SNIFF! SNIFF!*

Turn the page.

Freedom is forgotten. The buddies get on all fours like bloodhounds and follow the scent. It takes them to a staggering sight.

"Like, how did we miss this?" Shaggy gasps as he gazes up at a giant fairground tent that looks like a cupcake castle.

"Rit rooks rummy!" Scooby says. His mouth waters so much that it makes a pool of drool.

Shaggy looks to the left and right. He doesn't see any zombies chasing them.

"I suppose we could take a look inside," Shaggy decides.

Turn to page 96.

Velma is so surprised to see a zombie that she drops the torch. It hits the floor and goes out. She can't see anything, but neither can the zombie.

"If I keep very quiet, that creepy creature won't know where I am," Velma tells herself as she crawls across the floor. She can hear the zombie stumbling around in the pitch black basement. "Too bad I don't know where I am, either!"

Velma strains her vision against the darkness. Even wearing her glasses she can't see a thing. Suddenly she spies a glimmer of light.

"I hope that's the door to the kitchen," Velma whispers as she makes her way towards the dim glow.

Velma crawls on her hands and knees towards the weak spot of light as fast as she can. In her hurry her knee hits the fallen torch. **CLICK!** Suddenly its bright beam spears the darkness. Velma finds herself face-to-face with the zombie! Both of them jump back in surprise.

Turn the page.

"*Yaaa!*" Velma yells.

"*Yaaa!*" the zombie shrieks. The creature is so startled that it stumbles backwards into the wardrobe. It disappears down a hole with a lingering cry. "*Yaaaaaaa!*"

Velma picks up the torch and points it into the wardrobe. The zombie is gone!

"That's a very interesting vanishing act," Velma declares. "And as far as I know, zombies don't do magic. There's a mystery here!"

Velma peers into the wardrobe and looks around the inside with her torch. There is a hole in the bottom. The torch beam reaches only a metre or so before it is eaten up by darkness.

"I've read *Alice in Wonderland,* and this looks like a very odd rabbit hole," Velma decides. "I also know a clue when I see one."

Velma jumps down the opening. **SWOOOOH!** She slides down a metal chute and lands in an underground room. She also lands on the unmoving body of the zombie!

"Jinkies!" Velma exclaims as she scrambles to get off the ghastly ghoul. "Yuck! Yuck! Wait a minute, something's weird about this guy."

Velma runs her fingers over the zombie's face. Her expression wrinkles up in disgust.

Turn to page 99.

The roar of a revved-up engine echoes across the farmyard. ***VROOOM! VROOOOM!*** Fred is astonished to see the zombies are all aboard the old tractor. One of the creatures grips the steering wheel. It grins at Fred like a cat staring at a mouse it's about to chase.

"Uh-oh. It looks like that zombie is about to put its foot down," Fred says.

The tractor wheels spin in the dirt as the zombie driver accelerates. The huge back wheels spit grass and gravel out from under the wide tyre-treads. With so much traction in the back, the front wheels lift off the ground.

"I can't believe I'm seeing this! A zombie wheelie!" Fred exclaims.

"That gives new meaning to the expression 'popping a *monster* wheelie'," Fred observes as the zombies lean the tractor back on its rear wheels.

SCREEEECH! The driver finds the gear and accelerates the vehicle towards Fred. The exhaust belches black soot.

Turn to page 94.

"Someone needs to check that carburettor," Fred comments as he coughs in the cloud of stinky smoke.

The tractor zooms at Fred. He performs his own version of a wheelie as his feet spin in place. Soil sprays out in a fantail behind him as he digs out a rut in the ground. Suddenly Fred is five feet deep! He can't jump out of the trench in time.

"I'm doomed!" Fred gasps.

Fred watches as the tractor races towards him. For such an old vehicle it has enormous power. It also has a terrible driver. The monster misses Fred completely! The tractor skids in a tight circle. All but one wheel comes off the ground and the machine spins like a ballet dancer. **_WHAAAAM!_** It does not land like one.

The tractor and the zombies lie flat on the ground. Fred sees his chance to escape! He scrambles out of the hole he dug himself into and runs towards the orchard.

He has a plan. He'll hide in the leafy trees and watch where the zombies go.

"I'll follow them and get to the bottom of this mystery," Fred decides as he climbs up into the branches.

Turn to page 103.

Shaggy and Scooby go inside the cupcake castle tent. They enter a pastry paradise. There are shelves filled with cakes and tarts and pies of every kind stacked up to the ceiling.

"Like, pinch me, I'm dreaming!" Shaggy sighs. "Ow!"

"Hee-hee!" Scooby chuckles as he quickly hides his paw behind his back.

"Hey, I recognize these cakes. They're Whammy Grammy Cakes," Shaggy says. He looks around the tent. He and Scooby are the only ones there. "Do you think it would be okay if we had a little taste? You know, like, samples?"

Shaggy reaches out and takes a cake. Before he knows it he is balancing a huge pile of cakes in his arms.

"What are you doing here?" a voice demands.

"Zoinks!" Shaggy yelps and jumps in surprise as an old woman pops up from behind one of the shelves.

"Rit's a zombie!" Scooby wails.

Shaggy is so startled that the cakes in his arms go flying into the air. Scooby gobbles them up before they hit the ground.

"I'm not a zombie, I'm just a little old lady," the woman says.

Scooby-Doo isn't convinced at first. He sniffs the woman, and she smells of cake and icing.

"She smells rummy!" Scooby declares.

"It's not safe for you to be here," Shaggy warns the old woman. "There are zombies on the loose."

Suddenly a gang of ghouls rushes into the cupcake tent. Shaggy and Scooby shriek in fright, and their hair stands on end.

"Lady, look out!" Shaggy shouts.

"Oh, they won't hurt me," the old woman assures them. She cackles with hideous laughter. "They're my sons!"

Gruesome zombies surround Shaggy and Scooby. The old woman stands in the middle like their queen.

Turn the page.

"Meet the real Whammy Grammy family," she announces. All of the zombies take off their masks revealing unfriendly faces.

"Like, I should have known," Shaggy moans.

"I want to expand my cake business and need land to build a new factory. Bushytail Farm and the fairground are perfect properties," the woman explains.

"So your sons dressed up as zombies to scare people away and free up the properties," Shaggy realizes. The ghouls close in on the friends. "Wait! I have a last request. Scoobs and I want cakes as our last meal."

Before the woman can answer, Shaggy and Scooby become a tornado of food frenzy. They consume every crumb of cake, pie and pastry.

"You ate my entire stock! I'm ruined!" the woman wails. "You meddling kids!"

"Sweet victory!" Shaggy burps.

THE END

To follow another path, turn to page 11.

Velma kneels over the motionless zombie. She notices something about the creature that attracts her analytical eye. Velma reaches out and touches the zombie's face.

"*Ewww!*" Velma groans. An oily slime drips from her fingers. "What is this gunk?"

Before Velma can think about that, more zombies surround her! They grab her and drag her down a tunnel. This time Velma doesn't try to escape. She's curious. There is a mystery under Bushytail Farm, and she is determined to solve it!

Velma is taken to a small room and shoved inside.

"Velma?" a voice asks from the gloom.

"David!" Velma replies as she sees her missing friend tied to a chair.

"Am I ever glad to see you!" David says. "I've been kidnapped by zombies!"

Turn the page.

"There's no such thing as zombies, and I can prove it," Velma proclaims. "But there's something about Bushytail Farm that's so valuable that someone is willing to go to desperate measures to get it."

Velma tries to untie her friend. Her hands are slippery from the oily goo and she can barely untangle the knots.

"And I think I've just figured out what it is," Velma announces. "Follow me and I'll show you."

Velma and David sneak out of the room. She leads them deeper down the tunnel until they come to an amazing sight. David gasps!

Velma and David stand at the opening of a cave. There are a dozen short oil derricks inside the cavern, drilling for oil. Zombies work the drills.

"There's petroleum oil under Bushytail Farm," Velma says. She holds out her hands covered in dark goo. "This is the clue that solved the mystery. It's crude oil."

"You meddlers!" a voice grumbles.

Turn to page 102.

Velma and David turn to see a zombie behind them! Thinking fast, Velma uses the rope that once bound David and lassoes the creature. She ties a secure knot and pulls off the ghoulish mask.

"Uncle Mel!" David exclaims.

"*Bah*! I was going to force you to sign over the farm's mineral rights. And I would have gotten away with it except for that girl!" Mel confesses.

"Not just any girl, a member of Mystery Inc.," Velma says.

THE END

To follow another path, turn to page 11.

Fred hides in an apple tree and watches the zombies wobble to their feet. They lumber across the farmyard towards the orchard. Fred gulps as he realizes that the creatures are heading straight for him!

"Maybe this wasn't such a good plan after all," Fred shivers.

The zombies stumble up to the tree and stand directly below Fred's hiding spot. Then, they disappear!

"Where did they go?" Fred wonders as he leans over and hangs upside down from the branch. "Wait. There's something strange about the tree trunk."

Fred flips down to the ground to take a closer look.

"There's a door handle on this tree trunk! It must be a secret entrance, but to what?" Fred says. He grasps the handle and opens the door.

Fred discovers that the trunk of the apple tree is hollow.

Turn the page.

Inside, a ladder leads down into a deep shaft. There is a faint glow of light at the bottom. Fred cautiously climbs down the ladder. He stops before he reaches the base. He hears voices!

"Those Mystery Inc. kids are going to be trouble!" someone says. Fred can't see who it is. "We have to get rid of them or my plan is ruined."

"But boss, they're experts," another voice replies.

"Yeah. I've read about them and their adventures," a third voice states.

Hidden in the shadows of the shaft, Fred clings to the ladder and listens to the conversation. He decides that he has heard enough. It's time to act!

"Don't you know it's rude to talk about someone behind their back?" Fred says as he jumps down from the ladder and steps into the small room.

He sees the zombies and the farm's caretaker standing next to David, who is tied up.

"This isn't a mystery after all," Fred announces as he unties his friend. He points at the caretaker. "You're a disgruntled relative who wants revenge on David. You hired these guys to dress up as zombies to scare people away from Bushytail Farm."

"I told you they were experts!" a zombie says and takes off his mask.

"I had my own plans for the farm," the caretaker grumbles. "But now everything is ruined. I would have gotten away with it except for you."

"My farm is saved, thanks to Mystery Inc.!" David declares.

THE END

To follow another path, turn to page 11.

AUTHOR

Laurie S. Sutton has read comics since she was a child. She grew up to become an editor for Marvel, DC Comics, Starblaze and Tekno Comics. She has written Adam Strange for DC, Star Trek: Voyager for Marvel, plus Star Trek: Deep Space Nine and Witch Hunter for Malibu Comics. There are long boxes of comics in her wardrobe where there should be clothing and shoes. Laurie has lived all over the world. She currently lives in Florida, USA.

ILLUSTRATOR

Scott Neely has been a professional illustrator and designer for many years. Since 1999, he's been an official Scooby-Doo and Cartoon Network artist, working on such licensed properties as Dexter's Laboratory, Johnny Bravo, Courage the Cowardly Dog, Powerpuff Girls and more. He has also worked on Pokémon, Mickey Mouse Clubhouse, My Friends Tigger & Pooh, Handy Manny, Strawberry Shortcake, Bratz and many other popular characters. He lives in a suburb of Philadelphia, USA and has a scrappy Yorkshire Terrier, Alfie.

GLOSSARY

banister handrail that runs along a staircase

counterfeit something that is fake, but looks like the real thing

derrick tall, tower-like frame that holds the machine that drills oil wells

ghoul evil spirit or ghost, something that looks disgusting and death-like

inheritance money or property that are given to a person after someone dies

investigate to search in detail, to search for information about something

meddle to get in the way or to become involved in someone else's business

patent legal document that gives the inventor of an item the only right to make and sell it

reputation other people's judgment of something's quality or character

revenge the act of getting back at someone for harming you or someone you care about

YOU CHOOSE JOKES!

YOU CHOOSE which punchline is funniest!

What is a zombie farmer's favourite vegetable?
a. Head of lettuce.
b. Head of cabbage.
c. Head of Farmer Brown.

Why don't zombies like to eat dancers?
a. Dancers give them a ballet-ache.
b. Dancers give them toe-maine poisoning.
c. Dancers make them feel tutu full!

What does a zombie need to be a good farmer?
a. Dead-ication.
b. Ache-ers of land.
c. A skeleton and a head for starters, then he should be able to make his own farmer quite easily.

What did Shaggy say when he first saw the zombie?

a. "That guy looks dead tired!"

b. "I'd shake his hand, but I think it might fall off!"

c. "Why am I afraid of someone who doesn't have any guts?"

What kind of snack does a zombie farmer like to eat?

a. Chips and human bean dip.

b. Brain muffins.

c. Vanilla ice scream.

Why isn't Velma afraid of zombies?

a. "Zombies are nice – they like me for my brains."

b. She thinks they're super-ghoul!

c. Just like zombies, she likes having friends for dinner.

THE CHOICE IS YOURS!